on the ROX

I0742590

KAT ADDAMS

Copyright © 2020 by Kat Addams
All rights reserved.

Visit my website at: www.kataddams.com
Cover Designer: Lori Jackson, Lori Jackson Design,
lorijacksondesign.com
Editor and Interior Designer: Jovana Shirley,
Unforeseen Editing, www.unforeseenediting.com

No part of this book may be reproduced or
transmitted in any form or by any means, electronic or
mechanical, including photocopying, recording, or by any
information storage and retrieval system without the
written permission of the author, except for the use of
brief quotations in a book review.

This book is a work of fiction. Names, characters,
places, and incidents either are products of the author's
imagination or are used fictitiously. Any resemblance to
actual persons, living or dead, events, or locales is entirely
coincidental.

ISBN-13: 978-1-7331523-3-4

For all the women who have survived and especially for those who didn't.

WHILE THIS BOOK IS COMEDY, IT
CONTAINS A SLIGHT UNDERLYING THEME
ABOUT OVERCOMING DOMESTIC ABUSE THAT
MIGHT BE SENSITIVE TO SOME READERS.

ONE

Jay

What the hell?

I awoke to the sound of slamming car doors, hysterical laughter, and a faint bass line thumping from the unkempt home next door. I grabbed my robe, tied it around my waist, and shuffled upstairs to investigate this rude awakening. My body had finally adjusted to US time from Melbourne time, and now, this chaos would have me tired again. If I didn't get any sleep, I would not be productive at my new job tomorrow.

"I shouldn't have moved here," I mumbled to myself as I lifted my finger between the blinds of my guest room window and slowly peeked out toward my neighbor's home.

A line of cars trailed down his driveway. I shifted my feet and lifted the blinds higher. The music blared from his backyard, where a circle of people sat around a firepit. I squinted my eyes, trying to make out their shadowy figures. A tall, older man stood, talking with his hands. He circled his hips in a rude gesture.

That must be the bloody wanker who is my neighbor.

I watched his animated charade and listened to the laughter that carried up to me in my guest room as I stood to eavesdrop like a creepo. I pressed my free palm to my eyelid and rubbed. I was about to head back to bed to try to fall back asleep, but something—or someone—caught my eye. A beautiful, dark-headed woman, covered in tattoos, stood at a window directly across from me, staring straight into my guest room.

"Shit!" I dropped the blinds and took a step back.

Fuck.

I held my breath and lifted the blinds again. The woman still stood there, looking toward my window. I didn't have the best eyesight, but even from here, the view of this gorgeous moonlit goddess sent warmth tickling right up my spine, settling into my chest. My heart raced as she tilted her head to the side and put her hand to the window.

I kept as still as could be, watching her watching me. My breaths shallowed and softened as if she could somehow hear me and confirm that I was again spying on her.

She smiled out into the darkness and slowly slipped off her strappy dress, one shoulder at a time. I blew out a quiet breath and lifted the blinds even higher. She ran her hands up and down her body, pausing only to caress her petite breasts that fit snug into a black lace bra. Her leopard-print knickers didn't match, but I had the feeling she didn't care about such trivial matters, and neither did I. My cock thickened under my robe as I watched her swaying in front of the window, teasing me. She unclasped her bra with one hand, and with the other, she reached out beside her to flick the light switch off.

"Oh, damn it!" I muttered.

I stood at my window, waiting and wanting more. Finally, I puffed my chest out and gathered my balls to send the signal for her to keep going. I pulled the string on the blinds and opened them up entirely, waiting in the dark for her to return. Surely, she could see me standing in the night. The full moon basked my room in a soft blue glow, lighting up my pasty-pale arse wrapped up in a stark-white robe.

But she didn't come back. My eyes drifted down toward the man in the backyard. He moved about the yard, acting out a story and putting on a show, just as the woman had put one on for me. I desperately hoped that wasn't her husband or boyfriend or else I had moved next door to trouble. I pulled my robe around me tighter and sighed. I would need to go back to bed and rub one out before I could fall asleep again. Visions of the inked goddess moving her hips back and forth, teasing me, whirled in my head.

I reached up to close the blinds before the light in her window flicked on again, and there before me stood a gigantic inflatable T. rex.

I screamed and stumbled backward, falling on my arse. It wasn't my sexiest moment, but then again, neither was whatever the hell she was playing. I picked myself up, crawling back to the window, and peeked over the ledge. The T. rex gripped its sides with its tiny arms and threw its head back in sharp-toothed laughter. Her wide smile poked out from underneath the dinosaur's jaw as she laughed so loud that I swore that I could hear her voice.

I shook my head and smiled. T. rex made a humping dance and waved good-bye. I waved back, still confused over what had happened. I looked in the backyard again and watched as the dinosaur made its entrance into the crowd. The laughter grew wild.

Tomorrow, I would pick up earplugs and maybe even introduce myself to whatever crazies lived next door.

"Well, well, well. Look at what the kangaroo dragged in!" My brother, Aiden, clapped me on the back. "Let me show you the team."

I shook hands with everyone as Aiden introduced me to my new employees. I had co-owned five restaurants back home in Melbourne, but here, in the Southern states, the service industry was almost entirely different. People were a lot less laid-back, even in the South, which I'd thought was known for its drowsy state of mind.

"Ready to get started? I'll show you the ropes. You can tell me all I'm doing wrong," Aiden said.

He hadn't aged a day since the last time I saw him years ago.

"Ready as I'll ever be." I shrugged, following him to his back office.

He motioned for me to have a seat while he rummaged through his desk. "Now, now, you've had a two-year break! Traveling the world, eating just about every cuisine imaginable, and banging exotic women. Aren't you ready to settle down yet? You know the cuisine here is amazing—because I'm in charge of that—but the women here … well, I've never in my life met any like them. They don't grow them that way back home."

"Who said I was banging exotic women? Do you think there are arse-loads of exotic women down in the catacombs of Paris or the German war museums?" I set my laptop bag on his desk and plopped myself into a chair.

"Hmm. I guess not."

"Well, there are! I just didn't bang them." I folded my arms behind my head and leaned back, grinning at his mind-blown expression.

"What! Why the bloody hell not? You are tall, handsome, and have an Aussie accent. Do you know how many knickers I've gotten into just by my voice alone? I could say the stupidest things, and women hop right on me for a ride! I once told a woman how to bathe a monkey, and she unzipped my pants and gave me a blow job. She told me that I'd better not stop talking, so I kept on and on about bathing monkeys."

"What do you know about bathing monkeys?"

"Nothing, but it got my dick sucked, so I just said whatever the hell I could sputter out." He shrugged. "I'll take you out on the town this weekend though. Lots of things have changed around Outer Forks since you were here last. We'll go out, so I can give you a proper welcome. Let you whisper in some of these wild women's ears."

"Just how wild are we talking here? It's been far too long. I could use some fun, but I'm afraid my skills are lacking these days."

"How long is too long?" Aiden whispered as if anyone else could hear us over the loud noises coming from the kitchen. He finally found what he had been looking for in his desk and motioned for me to follow him back out into the hall, clutching a notebook in his hand.

"Two years."

He sucked in his breath. "Not since … Elena?"

"Nope."

"Mission number two: get Jay laid. Mission number one is still here. Help me get this thing off the ground, so we can open another on the other side of town. We're already doing pretty well, but you're the expert. I'm keen to hear your thoughts. Maybe you can bring some fresh ideas to the table. Literally." He handed me the notebook. "Here's a start. Look through this."

I nodded, taking the notebook and tucking it under my arm as we entered the kitchen through swinging doors. I glanced at the shiny appliances, the immaculate prep areas, the massive stoves. The familiar scent of charred meats, sautéing vegetables, and butter … lots of butter, and it gave me the first hint of comfort I'd felt in a long time.

"My thoughts right now are that Mum and Dad would be proud of you, brother."

"I think so too." He smiled. "It's good to have you home, Jay. Even if this isn't our true home, I'm glad you're back with me."

"It's our home now. A fresh start," I assured him.

The look of sadness that crept across his face disappeared into optimism as we made our way around the kitchen.

I spritzed myself with cologne before heading out the door and into my Uber. I hoped I would get lucky tonight. The last time I had touched a woman was a time I wished I could forget. Elena, my ex-wife, was a coldhearted ice queen. When I had tried to make love to her on our anniversary, she'd told me she ate too much at dinner and felt too bloated to mess around.

Never in my life had I ever felt too bloated to fuck. I had eaten so much at times that someone would practically need to roll me out of the restaurant, but rest assured, I could still fuck like there was no tomorrow. My dick worked under any circumstances—any and all of them, except one, and that had been the day after that failed anniversary. I had overheard her on the phone telling someone else—not me, her husband—that she loved them. That was the end of that chapter in my life. We had parted quickly and easily, going our separate ways that same day I found out. I hadn't known it then, but that was only the beginning of the worst week of my life.

"Good evening," the driver said as I buckled into my seat.

I politely made conversation, but my mind was stuck elsewhere. My nerves shook as I thought about how to let a woman know I was interested.

Should I wink?

Buy her a drink?

Tip my chin in the air?

Slide my finger back and forth into my other circled palm in a rude gesture?

I hadn't had to think of these things in what seemed like forever. The last time I had even glanced at a half-naked woman since Elena was that crazy lady next door—the T. rex.

I had slept upstairs in the guest room every night since she flashed me her lingerie—and her costume. My blinds remained open as I waited, hoping and maybe even begging. There was something about the way she had looked out into the dark and straight into my window that seemed familiar. She seemed familiar. Maybe she had been a guest at the restaurant before, but surely, I would remember someone as uniquely beautiful as her.

Even with her wild behavior and edgy tattoos, she reminded me of an exotic goddess. Not that I had anything against wild behavior and edgy tattoos. I only knew the calm and quiet type. I had grown up in a peaceful home with all of the traditional memories. My mother, Scarlett, and my father, Herb, had given everything to Aiden and me. There hadn't been many bad times back then. Not until the accident anyway.

At the end of my divorce week, Aiden had called one morning to tell me that our parents were involved in a car wreck after leaving their restaurant the night before. It was rare that they were ever apart, and my sole comfort from the whole tragic situation was that they had been together when it happened. I wouldn't believe in soul mates or any of that bloody divine-energy bullshit if it wasn't for my parents. They were perfect examples of what true love looked like in a relationship. Even after over thirty years together, they had never lost that sparkle in their eyes for each other.

I rested my head against the cold glass of the car window and wondered if I would ever find my person. My mind wandered into philosophical territory as I thought about the concept of soul mates. Sure, my parents were definitely each other's soul mate, but maybe humans didn't have only *one* person. Perhaps there were a lot of soul mates for us out there.

Better odds that way, I mused, taking comfort in my simple logic.

Although if there were lots of soul mates for me out there, I hadn't stumbled into any yet, and I had been everywhere. I had traveled the ends of the earth, and not once had I run into anyone who made my insides bubble up into my chest or my heart pound and flutter. I hadn't even felt that with Elena. She had been a safe pick for me—or so I'd thought. Her calm and quiet demeanor only hid something sinister underneath. I shivered in my seat, trying to block out how emotionless she had been toward the end of our marriage.

What a waste of my years.

Now that I was thirty-two, I yearned to settle down. I had done everything I wanted to do in life, except start a family.

"Will you be getting into any trouble tonight?" the driver asked, interrupting my pity party.

"I sure as hell hope so." I sat up in my seat and shifted my back, suddenly aware of my emotions showing in my pouty lips and furrowed brows.

"Well, it's poetry night at The Lounge. I'm not sure what kind of trouble lurks there, but it's probably eyeball deep in baggage and whining about smashing the patriarchy. You sure that is where you want to go?" he asked.

"Ah, poetry night sounds interesting. Maybe I'll learn something."

"Whatever you say. Just don't call me to take you home after a hippie with a man bun makes you cry and question your manliness—or worse, a woman."

What the fuck is wrong with this guy?

I wanted to teach him a thing or two about women, but I kept my mouth shut. I didn't have the energy to argue.

"Thanks. I'll be fine." I hurried out of the car as soon as he pulled up to the curb.

The neon lights of the bar's sign flickered in the dark.

"The Lounge," I muttered under my breath.

I stepped inside the dimly lit entry. The smell of alcohol that hung heavy throughout the hall beckoned me to come, sit, and make myself cozy with a whiskey. For a dingy dive bar that I would typically pass quickly by, I felt an odd sense of comfort as soon as I entered the building. I pushed my way through the narrow hall, packed away with the grungiest of people, and stopped in my tracks as soon as I reached the bar.

Straight across from me stood two inflated T. rexes onstage, reading aloud to each other. I instantly recognized the face of my neighbor. At least, I thought it was her. Her wide smile and dark eyes stared out from under a gigantic dinosaur jaw as she spoke to her friend, a woman whose skin was the same color as the way I took my coffee every morning.

Bloody delicious!

If the beauty from next door was taken, maybe her friend wasn't. I bit my lip and watched the two dinosaurs go at it, my dick stirring in my pants. I shoved my hands in my pockets and groaned. It had been far too long for me if dinosaurs were getting me going.

"Your claws dug deep," my neighbor said.

"Yours dug deeper," the other dinosaur added.

"You bared your teeth at me. Ready to pounce, making me small, insignificant, already dead inside."

"Extinct. You were extinct to me."

"And now, you are too." My neighbor reached around the back of her friend and let the air out of her costume, making a long-drawn-out hissing noise.

A crowded table in the corner rose to their feet, clapping and hollering as the two dinos hobbled offstage and toward them.

Aiden came up behind me, pulling me toward two empty spots at the bar, whiskeys already waiting. He leaned down to shout into my ear over the crowd's cheers, "I told you they don't make them like that back home."

"I'm not sure what I just witnessed." I ran my hand through my hair and shook my head, trying to make sense of everything.

"I'm not either. But you need to get laid, and this is the best spot. These women are crazy in bed. Also, maybe in the head. But you're looking for a one-night stand, right? Just a little fun to rev your engine back up."

I settled into my chair, sipping my whiskey and glancing at the table in the corner. The dinosaur stripped herself of her costume, confirming that she was definitely my neighbor. Her black hair fanned out over her bare shoulders. She wore a tiny sleeveless shirt and a skirt that left little to my imagination. I wondered if she hid any more tattoos under there.

"Earth to Jay! Where are you at? Don't tell me you're still jet-lagged." Aiden snapped his fingers in front of my face, bringing my attention back to the conversation.

"Right. No. Jet-lagged. Yes. I mean, yes, I'm pretty tired still from the moving and all. I probably won't be out long. I'm not sure I can swing a one-night stand on what little sleep I've had."

I returned my gaze to the corner table, searching for the man I had seen with her next door. He wasn't anywhere in sight. Only a group of gorgeous women sat around her table.

What kind of man wouldn't be by her side all the time?

I watched her laughing. Her smile lit up the dim corner, the room ... me.

"Really? Well, okay then. Let's just stay for a drink and a little more silliness. The later it gets, the more emotional the women get. But if you aren't yet ready to play the American field, we can wait. You're here now. You have the rest of your life."

"Yes, the rest of my life," I agreed, nodding toward Aiden but still watching my neighbor.

She and her friends began gathering their things. If she was leaving, she would walk right past me. I could either introduce myself or only get a closer look at her and be a total chickenshit. I opened my mouth as she passed, but my voice caught in my throat.

Chickenshit it is.

I locked my eyes on hers. Her perfectly arched eyebrows scrunched together as she sucked in her breath through parted pink lips. My heart plummeted into my stomach. Her eyes were dark as midnight and pierced straight through me like an arrow. A fucking cupid's arrow.

Wow. This whiskey and emo poetry are turning me into a big pussy.

I cleared my throat and shifted on my barstool.

"Do you know her?" Aiden nudged his elbow into my side as she disappeared behind me. "She was staring at you hard. Did you piss her off or something?"

"I think she's my neighbor." I looked behind me, hoping she would turn to look back, but I only caught sight of her perfect arse as the door shut behind her.

"The crazy ones with the loud parties that you told me about earlier? The reason you're too damn tired to get fucked tonight?"

"That would be the one. Wild and crazy. Isn't that what you brought me here for?"

"Well, yes. But a neighbor is too close for comfort. Don't touch that with a ten-foot stick—or dick."

"I'm not. I think she has a boyfriend or husband or someone else living there. I saw a man."

"Oh. Could be, or he could be a friend or something."

"Maybe. He looked old enough to be her dad. Plus, I haven't seen him but once, so I don't know." I finished my drink and rubbed my eyes. "I shouldn't have come out tonight. I think this whiskey is hitting me faster than I intended. I'm going to have to call it a night, brother. I'll rest this weekend, and next week, it's on. I'll be on the prowl. Maybe let's try somewhere else though. Somewhere more … me."

"Somewhere safer, you mean. With boring women who have trust funds, college degrees, and commitment issues, like the rest of the women you're attracted to."

"Don't push it." I laid my money on the counter and peeled myself off of the barstool before ordering my Uber.

My neighbor had rattled my brain, and I wasn't sure why. The look she'd shot at me as she passed by warmed my body just as much as the whiskey had. My entire being had heated up with her gaze. I hurried home to sleep in the guest room, blinds up, waiting to catch that look again. I needed to feel my body flush for her again. I made a mental note to introduce myself soon and find out if my mysterious neighbor was single or not.

Sunday brunch was our busiest time at the restaurant next to Thursday, Friday, and Saturday nights. To beat the morning rush, I needed to wake earlier than usual. I considered myself an early riser already at five a.m. when I usually set my alarm, so I could take a quick morning jog on the nearby hiking trails. The trails were a bonus when I'd previously scoped out homes to buy in Outer Forks. I needed my morning jog like I needed my cup of coffee every day or else I had trouble focusing.

My life reflection happened while my feet scrambled over the dirt paths. I huffed deep breaths of stress out of my lips and breathed clear, fresh thoughts into my mind. Running was therapeutic for both my mind and body. The tension melted from my shoulders with each exhale as I focused my thoughts on the good in people I had seen while traveling abroad.

I hadn't planned on taking off and leaving my homeland, but circumstances were right at the time, and travel was a life goal of mine eventually. I had only thought I would have the chance to do that when I retired. But after my parents' accident and Elena's betrayal, I was left with enough inheritance, time, and grief to fly away. I had packed my things the day after the funeral and told my brother, who was my roommate and the only family I had left, good-bye.

"How am I supposed to manage the restaurants alone?" Aiden asked, throwing his hands in the air as he watched me shove clothes into a backpack.

"Mum and Dad left us more than enough money to hire help. You can do it—or not. Sell them if you want. Go, live life. We're young, and now is the chance to do what we want. I'm not living the rest of my life here, detached—literally from the rest of the world," I answered, my voice shaking.

"I understand. I don't want to either, but Mum and Dad wouldn't have wanted to see their restaurants sold. I'm not doing that to them. Is that the real reason you're running, or is it because of that bitch, Elena?" He sat down hard on the edge of the bed, crossing his arms across his chest and sneering at the mention of her name.

"No. Yes. Maybe. I can't be here right now. I just can't. A door has opened, and I'm choosing to step through it. There's nothing left here for me. I'm not entirely stupid. I think about going back to Outer Forks and opening a restaurant, but that is after I get done traveling. I'll settle down then when I'm ready. Hell, maybe that can be a project for you. That is your ticket out." I zipped my bag shut and patted my pants pockets, making sure I had my wallet.

I tossed my keys to Aiden. "Here, take it. Everything. I'll help with whatever in any way I can while I'm traveling. Just let me know."

Aiden stood up, his eyes in line with mine. "I don't like this, but I get it, and I'll support you because you've supported me. You're my blood."

"Go with me then, Aiden. You can come too."

"But that's not me. I don't like to run, and you know it. I don't exactly want to stay here either, but I'll think about what you said —moving back to Outer Forks. I think Mum would have liked it if we ended back up in her old hometown. She was never impressed with the women here anyway."

"Let's be real. Mum was never impressed with any women we brought home. They were never good enough for us. 'Bless their hearts,' she'd say. What was that other thing she would go on and on about? The raven? She had some odd words of wisdom."

"She said the world was full of showy peacocks. Find the raven."

"Raven. I never understood it. Those are creepy birds."

"They're misunderstood, is all. They're extremely intelligent. They can trust and empathize. I think she was onto something, except showy peacocks are technically males, so I'm not sure she had her saying right. Maybe she meant a parrot or a cockatoo."

"I'd settle for a penguin at this point in my life. Anything other than those damn showy peacocks."

He laughed.

"Truth. I love you. I'll keep in touch, and maybe I'll be back and forth. We'll see." I embraced my brother for what I didn't know would be the last time in years.

Grateful didn't begin to explain how I'd felt when I saw the world. For two years, I had dined with monks in Scotland, worked a charity for the homeless in Italy, learned life lessons from an eight-year-old orphan in India, and met some of the most amazing and caring people. I found many ravens among the peacocks in the generous spirit of the human race. My dream and my life were now complete. When I had finally tired of living out of a backpack, I had known I was ready to settle, and Aiden's new adventure in Outer Forks had proven to be yet another perfect opportunity.

Despite my terrible last days in Australia, my life had almost been picture-perfect. It was my relationships that suffered. I had always been very predictable in the women I chose. I fell for the fancy feathers every time. My type of woman was a stamped copy of my previous girlfriend. Getting out of my comfort zone mentally and relationship-wise had been a more significant struggle than navigating the wide-open world. But taking a risk on someone so vastly different from me sounded like trouble.

My mind wandered to my edgy, inked neighbor. Just her looks alone were the polar opposite of the women I knew. None of my girlfriends, and especially Elena, even had one tattoo.

What could I possibly have in common with her? Why would I want to eat muffins in the morning with someone who demanded a slice of cheesecake?

Okay, that was a bad analogy. Someone who would eat cheesecake for breakfast probably knew a thing or two about living life fully, which I needed to learn myself despite my worldly experience. Cheesecake for breakfast didn't make sense in my logical brain, but neither did my attraction to the dinosaur next door.

I threw back the covers and pulled myself out of bed. If I didn't start my morning run now, Aiden would be all over my arse about being late for brunch prep, and I needed to run. Now. Last night's emotional roller coaster onstage still played on repeat through my brain. A part of me wanted to reach out to those women, but the other part of me wanted to run. Next time I tried to pick up a chick, I would need to find a place that served high tea with people who discussed lighthearted romantic comedies.

I wrapped my robe around me and stood at my window, peering through the purple-hued dawn and into the shut blinds of my neighbor. I wondered if the T. rex next door liked tea and romance novels.

TWO

Rox

"Rox! That guy is calling again! What do you want me to say?" Nikki held out her phone, shoving the screen in my face.

"Ugh! Tell him we don't need his business. We are doing just fine. If he wants the sauce, he can come to the truck and buy the damn stuff. We don't have time for a meet-and-greet with pretentious asshats!" I rolled my eyes and waved the phone away.

"Did you get that, mister?" Nikki smiled into the phone.

My jaw dropped. I hadn't known the poor guy wasn't on mute. I let it slide. So far, Nikki's attitude had brought in more business and not the other way around. People loved buying tacos from a team of mouthy women. This year alone, we had tripled our sales, beating out last year's record. We were all doing something right.

Did you seriously let him hear that? I mouthed, smacking Nikki in the butt with a dishrag.

She stuck her ass out for me to do it again. "Sorry. We aren't really into the whole white-tablecloth scene. Have you seen our truck? It's a pink taco truck with a giant taco on the top. I'm not sure our brand would jive with yours. You heard the boss; you can come buy some if you need some, but we are too busy for a sit-down to discuss logistics." She hung up the phone and shoved it in her back pocket.

"Thanks." I turned my attention back to the pan of simmering meat.

In two short hours, the dinnertime crowds would hit, and the last few days, we had sold out too early for my liking. We needed more prep and more food.

"You know, Rox, it might not be a bad idea to meet with him. If you don't want to do it, Betty would probably love to. We could test it out."

"Are you kidding me? Betty? She would walk into that meeting and have them—"

"On their knees. I'd have them on their knees and begging for the Shizzle," Betty spoke up from the front of the truck.

I rolled my eyes.

"And that is exactly why you aren't doing it. Layla either, and neither are you, Nikki. If anyone did it, it would be me. And I say, nope. Remember, if one of us disagrees with something, it's a no-go! Our hands are too full. We can't be making batches of the Shizzle Sauce for Scarlett Herb," I groaned. "Have any of you ever eaten there? It's a steakhouse. White tablecloths, a wine list for miles, and no free bread."

"When did you go there, Miss Fancy Pants?" Betty turned in her seat, looking up at me like I was full of shit.

I was. I had never been to Scarlett Herb or any extremely fancy restaurant. I didn't have the interest or the funds.

"I saw pictures on their website. I've never gone." I stared out of the open window and breathed in the chilled spring breeze. The cherry trees bent over in the wind, sending their petals into the air like a spring snowstorm.

"So, just because you saw pictures doesn't mean the owners or staff are pretentious," Nikki said, handing me a pair of goggles. Chopping onions was our least favorite part of working on the food truck. "He sounds nice on the phone! He has an adorable accent."

"I'm sure he is just peachy. But still, we don't have enough hands on deck to fill orders of Shizzle Sauce if we start to sell it as a side hustle. We don't even have the kitchen capacity to make more than what we use ourselves. Maybe in the future. Speaking of hands on deck, where the hell is Layla?" I asked.

"She called right before asshat Jones. Says she is running late. She'll meet us at our next stop," Nikki sighed. "That girl is an even bigger mess than me. Than all of us put together."

"Ha! Yeah, right! I think she is probably the smartest of the bunch—or at least, the most innocent. She needs to learn to use a calendar and a damn clock." I turned the stove off right before the meat charred—exactly how I liked it.

"The fuck? Innocent? She wouldn't be in DTF if she were innocent. *Dirty. Tough. Female.* Those are the rules. If Layla is innocent, then I'm a nun. And you know that ain't right!" Betty lowered her sunglasses and turned back around, strapping her seat belt over her cleavage. "Bitches, ready?"

"I guess we can finish once we get there. Where are we parking today? I can't keep track of this chaos." I secured our food, putting it away, and made my way to the front with Nikki.

"The square." Nikki tucked her goggles in a drawer and strapped herself into her seat.

"Seriously? But that is right by Scarlett Herb!" I protested. My fingers curled around my seat belt in a death grip as Betty pulled the truck out of the park and onto the main road.

"It's a sign." Nikki's eyes grew wide.

"Jeez! What am I going to do with y'all? It's not a damn sign. That's Thirsty Thursdays. People get drunk at the bars and want tacos." Betty shook her head. "It's not a sign. It's good business sense."

"Or it's a sign. Divine intervention. The universe is aligning us with Scarlett Herb because that side hustle is going to buy us a new truck. A Pink Taco Truck for every corner. We will own the whole damn town." Nikki snapped her fingers and wiggled her shoulders in a victory dance.

"Divine intervention, my ass. I'm not walking up to Scarlett Herb. They want us, and they can come to us. Besides, we already own the damn town," I called back to her, lowering my shades and smiling.

"Hell yeah! That's the spirit! DTF!" Betty cupped her hand around her mouth and shouted into an invisible megaphone.

"Hands on the wheel! That divine intervention is going to have to take the wheel if you keep driving like a bat out of hell!" Nikki shouted, grabbing the back of my seat.

"Don't you know I once dated a race car driver? I know what I'm doing. He taught me more than the dirty stories y'all done heard about." Betty revved the engine and sped off, pulling onto the interstate.

"Yeah, yeah. Hope he taught you how to get out of a speeding ticket." I looked into the side-view mirror, crossing my fingers that the police car riding our ass was only hungry for some tacos.

"Shit!" Betty's fingers gripped the steering wheel as she slowed to the side of the interstate. She rested her head on the seat and sighed.

"It's a dude! And he's young! Also kind of hot," I whispered, watching the officer walking toward us in the side-view mirror. "Pop 'em out, ladies! Hurry!"

Nikki leaned forward as we all wiggled our shirts down and pushed our boobs together. Betty didn't need to push anything together. There was no covering her chest up. It was just there, in your face, always.

"Do your thing, ladies. Maybe we can get back on the road fast and out of this ticket," I spit out right before the officer reached our window.

"Hello … ladies." He blushed, peering into our truck.

Oh yeah, this dude is going to be easy.

"Hey!" we answered in unison, smiling and sticking our chests out.

"Do y'all have any idea how fast you were going back there?" He cocked his head to the side as his eyes drifted between all three of our chests.

Fucking easy.

"It's my fault, Officer. I told Betty to speed up. We're trying to get to our destination, so we can turn our stoves back on. You see, I just made a batch of tacos. They are juicy. So juicy. I think these are the juiciest tacos ever made. If we don't get the ovens back on, they are going to dry out. No one likes a dry taco." Nikki leaned forward from the back, sticking her full lips out into a pout and twirling her hair.

"Is—is"—he cleared his throat—"is that right?"

"No, sir, no dry tacos here. We're always fresh and ready as soon as we open. You see, to position ourselves on top—of the food truck business—we have to be ahead of the competition. Everything is made in house and to order. Betty was just trying to get us to where we need to go, so we could finish what little prep work we have and keep the tacos juicy. Do you like juicy tacos, Mr. Officer? Have you ever eaten at The Pink Taco Truck? We have the best tacos in town," I said in the most innocent voice I could muster. I sounded like a schoolgirl at an all-boys band concert.

He pulled at his collar and sucked in his breath. His chest began to rise and fall faster and faster. "No, I haven't had the pleasure. Where will you be parked today? Maybe I'll swing by and get a taste."

I smiled and leaned down, showing him my full cleavage, which wasn't a lot—not sitting next to Betty Big Bags anyway.

"We'll be at the square today! Please come out. We won't disappoint." Betty grinned and licked her lips.

"On me. You're on me—us—it's on us. Lunch. I got you." I winked.

"I'll be there. And drive safe!" He patted the side of the truck and turned to leave.

We sat in silence until we heard his car door shut, and then we burst out in laughter.

"Easy-peasy." Betty laughed, beginning to pull back onto the road.

"We're so rotten! Think he really will be by? He was pretty hot … and that uniform! I'd serve him my juicy taco." Nikki sat back in her seat and inched her top back up and over her boobs.

"You'd serve just about anyone your juicy taco." Betty reached in the back and squeezed Nikki's knee.

"Nuh-uh! Not just anyone! I have standards, ya know!" She crossed her arms across her chest.

"Like what? As long as his pecker is as big as his thumb?" I laughed, leaning my cheek against the window.

"If y'all bring up the thumb incident one more time, I swear, I'll quit playing social media queen and put Betty in charge of our PR. Then, see what happens!" Nikki huffed.

"Well, shit. I'd better shut my mouth then." I grinned over at Betty.

"I'm still waiting on these standards." Betty raised her eyebrows.

"Rich. I'm easy."

"When the hell have you ever been with someone rich? I have seen all those ragamuffins you put out for. Wasn't Tony fresh out of jail and broke as fuck? He hadn't worked in years!" Betty laughed, slapping the steering wheel.

"Those were my old standards. New standards are different. I need a man who can take care of me. Maybe that sweet officer. That was divine intervention right there! My future husband!" Nikki sighed and put her hand to her heart.

"Officers are hardly rich." I shrugged my shoulders.

"Well, whatever. I can still fuck him. He was hot." Nikki threw her hands in the air and settled back into her seat.

"Mmhmm. We know you. He was hot! Better get on that one before I do. I like a man in uniform too, ya know." Betty fanned herself, still not putting both hands on the wheel.

"Oh, I'll get on it," Nikki assured her.

"Get it, girl!" I reached back to give her a fist bump. "Now, let's go sell some tacos and Shizzle!"

"Beep, beep, bitches!" Betty called out, flooring the gas pedal and hurtling us toward the town square.

The square bustled with crowds on Thursdays. Drink specials from the surrounding restaurants had people lining up and down the streets, especially in this perfect weather. Now that spring was in the air, every patio was full of diners. Most of everyone dined inside, but those customers who liked to drink did so outside. They sat in a prime spot to see our truck only a short distance away.

We pulled into the middle of the square, parking our truck directly across from Scarlett Herb.

"What?" Betty looked at me, jerking the parking brake up and into position. "It's the best spot, and you know it. Look, they already have a full patio. Those people are going to get drunk on their high-dollar cocktails and then not have money for their high-dollar food. That's where we come in. Cheap tacos. Drunk food."

I sighed, knowing Betty was right. I trusted her with everything. My friends were my family, but Betty was the nearest and dearest to my heart. She had stuck with me through the Tommy situation, no questions asked. She had stayed there for me, even when I kept going back to him, continuously building me up with the strength I carried so that I could finally leave his ass for good. The Pink Taco Truck had been born out of desperation on both of our parts. We had needed a better life, and we'd both worked our asses off to get it.

We had met while waitressing together at a downtown diner for years. On some of the slower late nights, we would mess around in the kitchen, making ourselves food, tacos specifically. We tried them out on a few customers, unbeknownst to our asshole boss, and they were a hit. A few more ironing out of the kinks in our recipes, and our taco truck came to fruition, thanks to our favorite customer, Earl. He bankrolled the business. He was a retired old bachelor with more money than he could spend. His generosity had saved our asses and set us on this new path in life. Earl was the only male member of DTF. We let the vagina requirement slide for him and only him.

"Sorry! I know I'm late. I got us something though! I think this is going to be good!" Layla opened the passenger door to the truck and shoved a bag in my face.

"What is this?" I took a large glass skull out from the wrapping and turned it in my hands.

"Skull vases. For these." She held up another bag full of flowers.

"We don't do flowers or anything cutesy." Betty narrowed her eyes down at Layla.

"It's not cutesy! I mean, come on! These skull vases are badass! I got them to go on a few tables I'd bought! Since it's spring, the customers might want to sit outside the truck. I thought—" Layla stopped mid-sentence and put her hands to her hips.

"It's a good idea. Let's try it. Show me these tables, and we can start setting them up. I have to finish prep with Nikki too. We're opening in about fifteen minutes. Let's go!" I smiled at Layla before shooing her away and hopping out of the truck.

"Flowers, Rox? Really?" Betty huffed out and shook her head.

"Well, at least they're in a skull. Let's just see how it works. I promise I won't let her put glitter on anything."

"I heard that!" Layla bounced past me, carrying a folding table.

"Good! Because if you bring glitter up in my truck, we are going to have problems. Big ones. Like *my foot in your ass* problems." Betty shut her driver's door and walked over to help Layla with the chairs.

"Promise. Plus, you got to admit, the chairs and tables are a good idea. I even got a few candles to put on them for when it gets dark!" Layla perked up.

Betty stopped walking and set the chairs down.

"Relax! They're black candles. Super dark and angsty. Just like you." Layla blew Betty a kiss.

"You're lucky that I love you. Otherwise, I would be making your skull into a vase." Betty shook her head and picked the chairs back up, positioning them into place.

"Can you two cut the shit and help us in here?" Nikki called from the window. "We don't have time for playing Martha Stewart. Tweets went out. Expect company in T-minus ten minutes!"

"Or less." I nodded toward a group of teenagers making their way to the truck.

"Coming, coming!" Layla shoved the flowers in vases and set them out on the tables.

Usually, four people in a food truck would be too much for me—or anyone. But when DTF got to work, we worked as one. Our seamless operation kept our business afloat and our customers happy. We worked well together in every situation, especially stressful ones. Each one of us had gifts ... and issues. But we laughed the bad memories away and focused on the positive. Nikki had even smudged our truck and ourselves with sage sticks to release any bad energy. I had smelled like sage for a week. To clear the negative energy in my life, I would need to bathe in it daily.

I wiped my brow with the back of my hand as I sat with a pen and my tattered notebook on a curb behind the truck. The night had been our most successful yet this season, and it would only be getting busier with the warmer weather.

"Rox?" Nikki came around the back of the truck, interrupting my train of thought. "More poetry? Is this a funny one or a deep one?" She peered over my shoulder.

"Deep."

"Oh." She sat down beside me and pulled me in for a hug. "I love you just the way you are," she said, kissing me on my forehead.

"Thanks, Nikki. I love you too."

"Do you? Because if you really did—" she started.

"Are you kidding me? Buttering me up for something, are ya?" I tapped the end of my pen on my paper and waited. "What do you need?"

"No. I really do love you. I just wanted to tell you that the man from Scarlett Herb is here, asking about the

Shizzle. He came to us, as you'd asked. Will you at least talk to him? Just hear him out?"

"Fine!" I rolled my eyes. "Send him around back and get the girls to start closing. I think we are out of customers tonight." I waved my hand in the air at the empty parking lot.

The streetlamps had turned on hours ago, and a hushed murmur drifted across the square from the only two restaurants that remained open.

"Yay! Okay! Also, he's hot, so ... you might want to take your hair out of that ponytail and fluff it up a bit. Come here." She leaned down, swiping a lipstick from her pocket and tracing it over my lips before I could protest. "Now, sell some Shizzle for us and get us that new truck!"

"I said, I'd hear him out only! What the hell?" I called to her as she bounced away.

I stood up, smoothing down my oil-splattered white T-shirt and readying myself to greet whatever hot, pretentious asshat had kept bugging me for my Shizzle Sauce when Scarlett Herb's owner peered from behind the truck.

We both gasped.

"Roxanne Corvus is it? Owner of the Shizzle?" came the sexiest damn accent from the sexiest damn man I'd ever seen in my life.

I peered back into eyes that were familiar, warm, kind, and not at all what I had expected.

"Yes," I breathed out. "Part owner. The girls and I work as a team. You can call me Roxie or Rox."

Or anything you want as long as you keep talking, I thought.

I looked him up and down, taking in his tall stature, his confident posture, his starched and pressed suit, and the perfectly manicured scruff that barely hid his chiseled jawline. But that accent ...

Oh, that accent.

"Rox." He grinned, the corners of his eyes crinkling.

The way he said my name sounded like a song that I wanted him to sing all the time.

Raaaaaawwwwwks.

A hot flash ran through my entire body and settled in between my legs.

What was that? A hot flash? I'm not even thirty!

I tried to gather myself, but my brain had quit working the moment he opened his mouth. My body felt funny, and my legs fought back the urge to run to this stranger, so I could throw myself on him. I wanted him to put his arms around me. I wanted him to whisper into my ear. I wanted him to taste my Shizzle. I would give it all to him. He could have it anytime and anywhere.

"Do I know you?" I cocked my head to the side and interrupted the awkward trance that we both couldn't seem to snap out of. "You look familiar. I can't say it's from Scarlett Herb though. I've not eaten there—yet."

"Aye. I'm afraid you do know me. I'm your neighbor."

"Wait! The new one … the one in the window?" I put my hand to my mouth as my jaw dropped.

This perfect man standing before me was the one who had been watching me that night. The one I played the trick on. I had barely been able to make out any of his features, only his shape in the window. My cheeks reddened as I remembered the humping dance I had performed while wearing the dinosaur costume.

"Yes." He nodded toward the back of the truck. "It all makes sense now. The T. rex stuff, poetry night."

He pointed at the mural Nikki had hired one of her friends to paint on the side of our truck. The T. rex was wearing lipstick and munching tacos with her tiny hands. Her claws were painted blood red, and her expression gave no fucks. We'd named her Rosie.

"Poetry night? You were watching me there too?"

"Yes, I was there last weekend. I saw you there and thought I had recognized you from under that costume."

He shoved his hands in his pockets and rocked back on his heels.

"I knew you looked familiar! That's where I recognize you from! I had no idea you were my neighbor though—or that ... oh my gosh. You saw me in my bra and panties! I'm so sorry! I might have been a little drunk that night!" I fanned myself with my notebook. I lied. I had been a lot drunk that night.

"Don't be sorry." He laughed, stepping closer to me. "It was a perfect show. I hope your husband wasn't mad that I saws you through your window. It's just that ... I was there because the noise had woken me. I didn't know you would be there, half-naked." His voice rolled off his tongue, making my toes curl, my brows twitch, my thighs spread.

I shuffled on my feet, catching the way he'd not-so-slyly asked if I was single.

"Husband? I'm not married."

"You're not? Oh. I thought I saw a man in your backyard, and I assumed—"

"Earl! You thought I was married to ... *Earl?* Eesh. Give me more credit than that. He's old enough to be my dad, and ... well, he is like a dad to me. Gross." I shivered.

He laughed in only a way a sexy Australian man could laugh; it was music to my ears. I wanted him to do that while he was inside of me. I wanted to feel his cock jump with every giggle as I clenched around him. This man already made me feel things I hadn't known existed and only in the matter of the few minutes that I'd met him.

Take my sauce. All of it. Take it. Take it, damn it.

I fought the internal battle in my head, digging my heels into the pavement to keep me from jumping in his arms and wrapping myself around him.

"So, you're single?" he asked.

"Yes."

Take my sauce. Me. Everything.

I clenched and unclenched my fist, holding back the weird convulsions my body ached to make as it tried to pull itself toward him.

"Perfect."

"What does that mean, perfect?"

He's perfect. Buy this damn sauce, so I can see you more often.

"It means, I'd like to hear more of this dinosaur poetry of yours, and I don't have to feel guilty asking. Not that I would ask a married woman out, but … I had planned to meet with you for business anyway. Except I had no idea you were … you. The woman in the window."

"Wait. Let me get this right. Are you asking me out? You just met me!"

"Yes, but I feel like I haven't."

His eyes searched mine, lighting up the entire parking lot. I'd never seen a sparkle like that in my life.

The hair on my arms rose as a slight chill shivered up my body. My heartbeat pulsed in my ears. This wasn't the same feeling I'd had in the past with panic attacks. This encounter with him felt like a happy freak-out, not a spastic freak-out.

"Let's get back to that in a second. I thought you came here to talk about Shizzle Sauce?" I continued.

"Aye. Shizzle Sauce. Shit. Sorry, I … you make me flustered. You're gorgeous, and I came over here, thinking I would meet someone who resembled a lunch lady. But you're no lunch lady, and I can tell you're someone I'd like to get to know. T. rex poetry and all. I'm new here. I could use some friends."

I tugged at the bottom of my dirty work shirt and narrowed my eyes. "Look here, buddy. I don't know what the hell that means, but in America, our lunch ladies will cut you for talking like that."

"I didn't mean to offend you! I was only imagining my lunch lady from my school days. I think she really was a witch. Mean as the dickens and a mole on the side of her nose with a hair growing on it and all."

I flinched. "Well, no, I'm not a witch. Not all the time. It depends on who I am dealing with." I crossed my arms, aware of how I looked—and smelled—after being inside a taco truck all day.

"Aye, I'm sorry. I think things are getting lost in translation. I'm not calling anyone a witch."

"What translation? You speak English."

"How's this weather out here? Perfect, isn't it?" He threw his arms up, motioning around the dead square.

"Just peachy. Back to the Shizzle Sauce." My voice fell flat, but I still would jump his bones.

"Or the date?" He lowered his voice and took a step closer to me.

My chest tightened as my heart struggled to beat its way out of my rib cage. I could hear it thumping in my ear, and if he stepped any closer, he could probably hear it too.

"You'd date a lunch lady?"

"As I said, you're no lunch lady. You're … the most beautiful woman I've seen since I've been in the States. You're gorgeous. Even in a T. rex costume. I thought so that night I saw you in the window and at The Lounge. I just figured you were taken. How could someone like you not be?"

I put my hand to my chest and fluttered my lashes down. No one had ever said anything like that to me before. The best compliments I'd received were that I was hot as fuck or bangable. Never gorgeous, beautiful, smart, or any of that other stuff I wished I had been called.

"I don't mean to be abrupt. That is how we are over there. I can tell you all about it if you'd like. On that date perhaps? And we can talk Shizzle too. We can call it a business meeting, if you prefer. Just as long as I can hear more of this poetry, sneak that in there somehow."

"You haven't even told me your name." I shook my head.

"Oh my. You really do frazzle me. How rude of me. I'm Jaxon. Jaxon Taylor, but you can call me Jay. A pleasure to meet you." He stuck his hand out.

I took it in mine and tried to firmly shake it in my best business handshake, but I failed miserably. I let my hand hang there and gave him a soft squeeze. Our palms made a farting noise, causing me to quickly jerk my arm away.

"Well, that's never happened to me before." He scrunched his brows and tapped his chin. "Let's try that again, shall we?"

Fuck, he sounded so prim and proper and oh-so damn sexy. Pretentious or not, I didn't care anymore. I needed him to keep talking.

I straightened my back, pursed my lips, mentally quieted my embarrassment, and stuck my hand out, remembering that I was a boss babe and this man wanted my Shizzle Sauce.

Take it all. Me. Take me. Straight to bed. With our farty hands and all. Let's go.

"There we go." The corners of his mouth turned up into a smile as he shook my hand, not letting it go.

World's longest handshake, but I didn't care. I clung back to him. Whatever we were doing was sending warmth throughout my entire body and a spark between my legs. If he was this good at a handshake, I wondered just how good he would be in bed.

"Jay," I breathed out his name. "The pleasure is all mine. I'm sorry I haven't been available to take your calls."

I reluctantly pulled my hand back and tucked a stray hair behind my ear. I should have put my hair down for this. Nikki had warned me, and I didn't listen.

"My brother, Aiden, the other owner of Scarlett Herb, is the one who's been calling you. But it will be me from now on." He winked.

Fuck. There're two?

"Oh. Okay. We've just been so busy lately."

"That's okay. We're pretentious arsehats who don't jive with your brand." He raised his eyebrows as I shifted my eyes to my feet.

"About that—" I stammered.

"Ready to roll, Rox?" Betty stuck her head out of the driver's window.

I didn't notice that everything had been packed away.

"Just one second!" I called back.

"Let's talk about it over our date. I'm keen to hear your thoughts and that poetry."

Keen. Why can't American men use that word? It sounds so … fuckable.

"Date, business meeting—whatever you want to call it, yes, I'd love to. Just don't bring up the T. rex incident in the window, and I'll be good."

"I might not want you to be good," he whispered.

Whoa. He must feel this chemistry too.

"Perfect, because I'm usually not." I shrugged, smirking and heading toward the front of the truck. "Not this Saturday, but next. Seven o'clock, The Lounge bar. You know the place," I called out to him before quickly disappearing into the truck. I took a few deep breaths and tried to steady my breathing.

"What the hell was that? And why do you have that pep in your step? Why are you breathing funny? Did he slip you some money or drugs or something? I've not seen you bounce around like this before. You okay?" Betty started the engine and sat back, waiting for me to explain before she would leave.

"Divine intervention," Nikki chimed in from the back. "I told you! It's all these crystals I've been hanging around here!" She pointed toward the crystals that were tied down to everything from the front to the back of the truck.

I watched out the window as Jay walked back to Scarlett Herb. He had a pep in his step too.

"Maybe so. But I have a date, and we might be moving on up in the world if we partner with them," I answered.

"So, let me get this straight. Jay owns Scarlett Herb, he asked you out on a date, and you just all of a sudden want to give him our sauce? After we've been telling you to do this all along? Sounds about right." Betty shook her head and pulled out of the parking lot.

"Well … did you hear him talk? He has an Australian accent. I'm not going to turn that down!"

"Oh, really? No, I didn't hear him. But maybe I should turn around and listen. I guess I'll have to agree with you on that then. I probably couldn't have resisted either. Glad we are moving forward with it though. I think it's a good idea." Betty shrugged her shoulders.

"Hope so. His accent is hot as fuck! And so is he." Nikki nodded from the backseat.

She was waving around a crystal in the air, probably clearing some type of energy. Bad luck, I hoped. I was full of that.

"He has a brother," I said. "He is the other owner."

"Dibs!" Betty sputtered out, snapping her fingers in the air.

"That's fine. I got a hot date with that officer anyway. I passed him my number when I gave him his receipt, and he is texting me now!" Nikki set her crystal down and smiled into her phone.

"What about Layla? Maybe she wants a shot at the brother from Down Under too." I raised my eyebrows at Betty.

"She ain't here, so … nope. Well, maybe. Let me get a glimpse of what he looks like first. If he looks like a turd on a stick, hard pass. You can report back to me once you meet him."

"I think I'm only working with Jay now, but I'll let you know what he says about the Shizzle Sauce. I'll run it by all of you before we start collaborating. DTF is a team." I leaned my head back and closed my eyes, still picturing Jay in my mind.

I'd never had anyone in my life throw me off-balance so quickly, and now that I was headed home, he would be there—right next door. My heartbeat quickened again.

"Oh, and another thing. Jay is my neighbor," I muttered, still smiling. I brought my hands to my cheeks and felt my smile, confirming that I hadn't imagined it. It had been a long time since I smiled like this.

Betty and Nikki both gasped.

"Of course he is, that's just your luck. Pretentious restaurant owner turned hot-ass Australian lover lives right next door to you. I don't think that is necessarily bad luck, but it probably isn't good either!" Betty laughed, hugging the steering wheel.

"I'm telling you. It's divine intervention. All of this is." Nikki shook her crystal in the air again.

I thought about the way he had been there that night at the poetry event, how he'd watched me in the window back at home, how he'd tried to connect with my business, how it had been him everywhere and appearing suddenly out of thin air. I just hadn't known who Jaxon Taylor was yet. Maybe there was something to all of this mumbo jumbo Nikki droned on and on about.

"Give me that." I grabbed the crystal out of Nikki's hand and stuffed it in my bra.

"Lawd help us all. Maybe you should stuff it somewhere else, too, if you're looking to get laid." Betty wiggled her brows at me.

"That works too! Don't ask how I know!" Nikki smirked, not looking up from her phone.

"We won't," Betty said. "But you'd better give me one too. Just in case."

THREE

Jay

I opened my windows, letting in the fresh spring breeze. I took the day off from Scarlett Herb to unpack more boxes and run errands for essentials that I still needed. My home didn't even come close to beginning to feel like a home. Instead, it felt like a rather large storage unit—packed full and extremely disorganized. I preferred things orderly and tidy. This chaotic mess kept me from what I wanted to do—invite Rox over after our date night.

I sat on my smooth leather couch that had been delivered yesterday and leaned my head back, rubbing my palms up my cheeks and through my hair. Moving in and of itself was exhausting, but moving from the other side of the world was the worst. I flipped absentmindedly through the calendar of my phone and set it down beside me. I still had days to go before my date on Saturday, and I needed to see Rox again already.

I had waited nightly for another peep show, but so far, I'd barely seen her. The other morning, I had caught a glimpse of her running to her car, coffee in hand. I'd also heard her car door slam the other night and peeked outside, watching her check her mail well after midnight.

I felt like a creeper, a stalker, a loon. But I couldn't stop. Rox had set up residence in my brain, and I couldn't put my finger on why. She wasn't like girls I usually dated. Most of my ex-girlfriends and even Elena had been much, much different. They had no tattoos and wouldn't be caught dead in the pair of Chucks Rox fashionably pulled off. My exes ate salads with kale, drank only chardonnay from Napa, played tennis on weekends, and highlighted their hair with the seasons. That was my type—or at least I'd thought it was.

But the second I'd laid eyes on Rox, I'd felt different. Comfortable even. Her body was a canvas, decorated with stories I wanted her to whisper into my ear. Those dark eyes fluttering as she crawled on top of me, pressing her soft lips into mine.

I looked around my den, shrugged my shoulders, and pulled my hard cock out.

I might as well clear my head so that I could get back to work.

Now is as good a time as ever, I thought to myself.

What better way to procrastinate unpacking than rubbing one out to the sex-kitten neighbor?

The story seemed familiar as I remembered a porno clip I'd watched one time. Horny neighbors. I could dig it.

I ran my palm up and down the length of my shaft, leaning back, closing my eyes, and biting my lip. Rox's smile played in my head, precisely what her smile would look like while wrapped around my dick. I would brush her hair back from her eyes and gather it in my hands as she worked me with her tongue. Her slight Southern accent would twang softly in her moans. I wanted to pull her up and guide her down onto my bed, knocking her knees apart with mine and shoving myself in between them while I lifted her skirt. Her white Chucks still on, hitting against that little spot behind my knees, tickling me, making my cock jump right before I plunged inside of her.

Ding-dong!

The doorbell rang out, echoing off my empty walls.

I absentmindedly choked my chicken—really choked it—strangling the life out of it as I grabbed my dick hard from being startled or seen. My blinds were open, and I was stupidly sitting right in front of them. Of course, whoever the hell had interrupted me could look through any second and—

She did.

Rox knocked on my window, cupped her hands around her eyes, peered inside, and locked eyes with me, and then—*boom*—I somehow came. Fear shot through my veins as my hot load shot off, too, like a rocket sputtering out in forever squirts that just. Would. Not. Quit. This had never happened to me before. Sure, I'd heard of people messing their pants from fear. But I had never heard of coming in your pants—or worse yet, all over myself and my new couch while my hot neighbor watched. Yep, I had definitely seen this in a porno before.

I only had a few moments to think of how the hell I could recover from this—and I couldn't. Rox had hopped away from the window at my first spurt of dick tears, and at this point, I wouldn't be surprised if she had already put her house up for sale and was long gone.

Ding-dong.

The doorbell rang again.

I sat stupidly with my dick in my hand, unsure of what my next move would be. I couldn't ignore her forever.

"I'm coming!" I called.

"You already did!" she called back, not missing a beat.

Fuck!

I ran to the bathroom and grabbed towels, cleaning myself and changing my shirt before sopping up my mess on the couch. I clenched my jaw and shuffled my feet to the door. I took a deep breath, cried a little inside, and opened it.

"Rox … I wasn't expecting anyone. I'm—did you …"

"Did I see you christen your home with your own Shizzle Sauce? Yes, yes, I did." She pressed her lips together, struggling to keep it together.

"Yeah, I'm—wow. Holy hell, I'm humiliated. Can we not talk about this ever again? I'm so sorry you had to see that! I'll keep my blinds shut from now on. Lesson learned." I saluted her. No idea why I'd saluted her. I was fuzzy from endorphins, stress, and a load that I thought had emptied not only my balls, but my brain too.

"Look, let's forget what happened. We are even. We're both Peeping Toms. Here, take this." She held out a bottle of champagne. "*Welcome to the neighborhood* gift. Fitting as, now, I know you like to pop your top all over the place."

"I thought you said we would forget that ever happened!" I cringed and took the champagne, death-gripping the bottle and mentally kicking my ass.

How stupid was I to yank my crank in broad daylight in front of a window that I now wanted to black out forever?

"I'm teasing! Anyway, I, uh, know you're busy. So, I'll let you get back to work." Her eyes twinkled, and her mouth twitched.

"You're not going to let this go, are you?" I shifted my weight to one foot and choked back my shame.

"You're already getting to know me so well, Jay."

"Sounds like I'm in for a wild ride." I raised my eyebrows and held up the bottle of champagne.

"You've no idea." She bit her lip, hesitated, and stepped back. "Anyway, hey! What's your number? Text it to me and I'll text you back mine. That way you can text me on Saturday when you arrive. It tends to get packed on those Saturdays. Wouldn't want to lose you in the crowd."

"What does that mean, those Saturdays?"

"It's the Saturday for the women and children's shelter. We raise money for them." Her voice grew soft, and her eyes glazed over.

"We?" I shifted my weight to my other foot, confused.

"Me and the girls. We volunteer for the shelter. Once a month, we hold a benefit at The Lounge. So, you'll be supporting a good cause."

"Wow! I'm impressed. Count me in. I'd be delighted to do that." I watched her as a smile crept across her face, crinkling her eyes, and it sent my heart plummeting down into my stomach. She might be a tough cookie on the outside, but she had a heart of gold. "Did you want to come in for a minute? It's a bit dirty in here and—"

"I can't. But thanks. I have to run. Enjoy the champagne, and welcome to the neighborhood."

She turned to leave but came running back for my number. I gave it to her, thanking her again for the gift. Her sweet arse bounced as she walked away.

Saturday couldn't come soon enough.

Aiden and I had been working at the restaurant from morning to late at night over the last few days. We had hired three new employees, including a marketing assistant with the good sense to post on social media a special offer on a new craft cocktail. It'd brought us in twice the amount of customers we usually served on a Friday night.

When business finally slowed down, I sat at the bar and asked our bartender, Terrance, to make me one of these already-famous concoctions.

"Fleur-de-lis." The bartender nodded toward my glass. "That's what makes it so special. It's the rum. Straight from NOLA."

"Oh, wow. It is delicious! Good job, mate! Can't wait to see what you come up with next!"

"Thanks." He slid into a dance, working his way to the other side of the bar where two beautiful women paid their bill and gathered their things, all the while flirting with him.

"Jay! Rough night, aye?" Aiden sat beside me, scooting his barstool closer and motioning Terrance back over for a drink.

"Rough but successful. I don't think we have had a crowd like that before, coming in for only drinks. Must be those tweets. Never understood what the big deal was about that social media stuff, but I guess I get it now."

"You've always been such an old soul," he said, leaning into the bar and rubbing his eyes awake.

"It's hard to keep up with this fast-paced world; that's all." I rubbed the back of my tense neck, thinking about the hot shower I would take as soon as I walked through my door.

Aiden and I drank in exhausted silence. The last customers hobbled out of the restaurant, and the servers slowly filed out behind them too.

"Hit the road, Terrance. We got it from here," Aiden said, standing up and making his way behind the bar.

I watched Aiden begin to clean up and shut everything down, halfway feeling guilty for not offering to help but halfway too damn tired. No matter what I had tried, my nights here were sleepless. I tossed and turned every evening.

"Why did you want the Shizzle Sauce?" I asked as I rested my head in my hands.

"Whoa, that is out of left field. I thought we gave up on that."

"No. I didn't. I checked them out last week. Roxanne, the owner, agreed to meet to talk about it. I need to know what exactly we want it for, so I can let her know."

"Really? Why didn't you tell me this? And how did you do that? I've been trying to connect with them for the last few months! All I ever get is some snarky lady with a sharp tongue, pretty much telling me to fuck off."

"Well, that's why. You need to present yourself. Be personable. I walked over there and introduced myself, and that was that. We're meeting for a date-slash-business meeting on Saturday. I'm only curious as to what we'd even do with it. It doesn't seem like our normal offering."

I ran my palms along the underside of the carved wood bar before leaning onto my elbows and waiting for my brother to explain.

"It's not. But I want to try something new—local infusions. We're a fancy steakhouse. We need something to separate us from the dozen others around here. I want to incorporate other local businesses as much as possible. We already use local farms and bakeries. But we've never collaborated with another food vendor—especially a food truck. Maybe those people who think we are pompous assholes will see that we can also be down-to-earth. Supporting the little guy."

"That sounds like more of an idea from me than you! I like it. But have you met her? Roxanne? She's hardly a little guy. None of the women who work that truck are. I think if you called them that, you might have your balls sent back to you in one of your fancy to-go bags."

"Really?" Aiden stopped wiping the counter with the dishrag. I could see his brain working overtime, trying to connect the dots and the risks. "Are they single?"

"Roxanne is. But dibs. I don't know about the rest. I'm sure you will meet them if we can come up with a plan for working together."

"You're the talker, the consultant with the brains. I'll trust you on that. Throw me a bone though if you see one. American girls," he growled, continuing to wipe up the spills on his expensive-as-fuck bar.

"Not just American. Southern and from Outer Forks." I laughed.

"Mum always wanted us to meet a Southern girl like her. She would be so proud if she knew where we were at now."

"Yep, she would. She would bless our hearts." My laughter faded out into a heavy silence.

"Come on. Help me finish up. Let's go home. You've got a big date to get ready for tomorrow. Give her some of your sauce, and maybe she will give us some of hers."

I pushed myself off of my barstool and groaned. After my soaking explosion in front of her, I wasn't sure I had any sauce left to give.

I readied myself for my first date in years by doing what I did best—again cranking one out. If her gaze alone could make me come in my pants, I wasn't risking if she accidentally brushed up against me. I could only imagine how her skin would feel, sliding against mine. I thought of her hovering above me, our faces framed with her dark locks. That mischievous grin of hers sent my cock into instant spasms.

I heard the familiar slam of her car door as she pulled out of her driveway. I'd already become used to the way she shut her door, all loud and with no care at all. As if she wanted her neighbors to know that Rox was home and they'd better watch out. Over the past week, I'd come to learn her routines. She screeched out of her driveway a little after seven in the morning on workdays. Sometimes, she would circle back and run inside and grab something she'd forgotten, usually her coffee.

I would sip my coffee in the morning, looking out over the kitchen window and watching her go. The way her hip bones peeked out from her low-slung jeans when she bent over was enough visual to help me start my morning off right. The slightest hint of a tattoo showed on her lower back, and I ached to discover just what it was one day. Sometimes, I would hear the loud rumble of The Pink Taco Truck idling in her drive, right before three quick and rude honks, which always jostled my nerves.

The woman in the driver's seat would stick her head out the window, calling to Rox, "Good morning, sunshine!"

But my favorite part of hearing that car door slam was at nighttime. The sound it made was a much slower, exhausted slam than the frantic morning commotion. When I heard her slam that door, I knew she was home safe. I had only been at home to hear it twice last week, but when I did, I'd scurry up my stairs, hide in the shadows, and peer out my window. I'd mentally trace her steps throughout the house by each light that flickered on. What I imagined was her living room light would flip on first, followed by a kitchen light, and finally, the room upstairs.

Sometimes, I would catch her glimpse out the window and into mine. Of course, this sent my body shamefully barreling backward every time. I didn't want her to think I was a stalker because I wasn't.

Am I?

There was something about Rox that drew me to her as I'd never been attracted to anyone before, and yet I couldn't put my finger on it. She was just so … different than my norm.

Every time the lights turned off in her room, I would lie down in my bed and imagine what it would be like to be lying beside her—and not just fucking either. I wanted to hear her breaths slow and soften as she drifted off into sleep. I wanted to wrap her up in blankets, putting my nose to the back of her neck to breathe her in.

I wanted more than sex with her, but the hint of hesitation I'd heard in her voice when we last spoke let me know that she was, for some reason, cautious of me. I probably shouldn't have watched her peep show that first night—or at least, I shouldn't have let her know I was watching it … and enjoying it.

I sighed, cleaned myself up, and ordered my Uber. If I planned on getting laid tonight, I would need a drink or three. I had been out of the game for far too long.

I double-checked my reflection in the mirror and made sure that I wasn't too overdressed for The Lounge. That first night I'd been there, I'd felt like a fish out of water in my tie and sports jacket. Aiden hadn't bothered to tell me the bar had an atmosphere of dark, gloomy, and grunge.

Figures.

I straightened my shirt, tucking it in and out several times before finally settling on tucking it in for good. I wanted to be myself, but I didn't want her to keep thinking I was a pretentious arsehat either. I ran my fingertips through my hair with a tiny dab of gel, spiking it messily on my head instead of my usual prim-and-proper look. I even became ballsy and unbuttoned the top two buttons of my shirt.

Satisfied, I winked at myself in the mirror and even blew my reflection a kiss. Again, the endorphins—and Rox—were making my brain fuzzy. My phone dinged in my pocket, alerting me that my ride would be here in a moment. I hurried out the door and braced myself for a date with the wild woman next door.

I made my way to the same back corner table where her group of friends had sat at the last time I was here. I elbowed my way to her, the dark-headed goddess who had mysteriously cast me under her spell. Even here, in the dim light, she lit up that dark corner like a single golden ray of sunlight. Everyone else around her faded to black.

"You made it." She stood to greet me and smiled. "Jay, I want you to meet Betty, Nikki, Layla, and Earl. We're all owners of The Pink Taco Truck."

"Pleased to meet you." I gave a little wave at the curious eyes staring back at me.

"The pleasure is mine!" Layla jumped up out of her seat and took my hand, shaking it. "That accent! Wow. Are you French?"

"Calm down, sugar. Don't you know a British accent when you hear one?" Earl groaned, rising to his feet to reach across the table and introduce himself properly.

"Actually, I'm from Australia. But that's all right. We are a bit like Texans with British accents. Close enough, I suppose." I shrugged my shoulders.

"Down Under, eh?" Nikki twirled her cocktail straw before pulling it out of her drink and sliding it sideways between her lips, wetting them. "Sounds … interesting. I heard men from over there are wild. Great outback and all. You guys like to do it all. Wrestle gators, trap bears with your hands, wring a snake's neck."

Wring a snake's neck? I wondered if Rox had told them about me jerking off.

I looked around for a waitress. The time to start drinking had come.

"We don't have bears, but—" I started.

"Nikki! Why are you stereotyping this poor man? Jeez Louise. Welcome to 'Murica, Jay man. Be prepared to be stereotyped." Betty rolled her eyes.

"I, uh … that's okay. I don't think Americans know a lot about Australia. Your school systems don't—" I began before noticing each pair of eyes snap to me.

The ladies' postures prickled. Earl sat back, nodding.

"Let's go over here where we can discuss business, Jay." Rox pulled me away to a tiny, empty table far enough not to hear the conversation coming from the taco truck gang but close enough so that I could still see them scoping me out.

"Did I say something wrong?" I pulled her chair out for her.

"What are you doing?" She stood, glancing at me and back down to the chair.

"What do you mean, what am I doing? Pulling your chair out? Am I doing something wrong again? Is there some cultural thing in America I don't know about? Please tell me. I don't want to offend anyone. It's not my intent. No use in getting started on the wrong foot. Do I need to tuck it back in? I know you can do it yourself and all. I can't help it. Comes naturally. Gentleman until the end."

I grabbed the back of the chair again, ready to push it forward before she put her hand on mine, stopping me. The warmth of her palm sent a spark up my arm and into my gut, punching it and knocking me out of breath.

"No, no. You're fine. It's fine. I'm just not used to chivalry, is all." She lowered herself into the chair and tapped the one next to her, beckoning me over. "Start talking Shizzle." She smiled up at me.

I slowly breathed again, realizing I had been holding my breath since she touched me.

"Let's get down to business, of course. We hope to open ourselves to more local markets—the smaller ones. We want to serve your products in our restaurant. We realize it is a big undertaking, given you work on a small scale and we are much larger, but we would like to offer you our kitchen for prep. Also, we would buy it outright from you, so we don't have to worry about profit sharing."

"What would your steakhouse use Shizzle Sauce for? You guys don't have tacos. I can't imagine anything on your menu meshing with it. I'm just confused. It's weird."

"Braised pork belly. We're thinking about offering a few select entrées featuring some of the more popular local items. Your Shizzle Sauce is shouted out from every social media platform known. People love your style, your food, your menu, you. We don't only want to be thought of as … what did you call us … pretentious arsehats?"

"I see. You want more of the local scene. Something Outer Forks. What does an Aussie know about Outer Forks?" She folded her arms across her chest and leaned back. Her long, dark locks spilled over her shoulders, down to her elbows.

"My mum was from here. We spent a lot of time back and forth, growing up. Dual citizenship. It's just been a very long while since I've been here." I cleared my throat, mentally thanking the waitress who interrupted us to take our drink order.

"Beer. Anything on tap. Something local, please," I chimed in, noticing the corners of Rox's mouth turn up.

"Local beer it is for me too, Sal." She winked at the waitress. "Now, you were saying. Your mom lives here?"

"Lived." I rubbed my palms down the thighs of my jeans and turned my attention toward the stage. My knee bounced steadily under the table.

"Oh. I'm sorry," she said, barely audible.

"For?" I looked back at her.

Her long eyelashes fluttered down as she reached across the table and squeezed my arm. Electricity. The sparks from her fingertips sent the hairs on my arms standing at attention.

"Your loss."

"How—"

"Because I'm me. And I've been through a lot. And I can recognize pain when I see it." Her eyes were no longer focused on me but in the distance toward the stage. "These women you're about to see, they all have that talent too. Watch." She nodded at the lady who stood at the microphone onstage, clutching her paper in a death grip and looking out over the crowd.

I listened to over an hour's worth of poems as I sipped my beer and became uncomfortable as fuck. Every few minutes, a new woman would step up onto the stage and pour out her life for all of us to see, but to my surprise, the room wasn't full of sniffles and tears. Some of the poetry was a riot, but most of the poems ripped my soul to shreds. Still, despite the sadness, the atmosphere in the room was positive, uplifting, and female—almost all females. My balls shriveled in my pants.

"What do you think?" Rox nudged me with her elbow.

"I think there isn't enough beer in the world to make me feel better about my species." I shook my head.

"I think we've found something in common then. Bottoms up!" She clinked her bottle to mine.

"Cheers, mate! Do you really do this every month?" I tipped my beer back, turning my body to face her during an intermission.

"Every. Single. One. The Pink Taco Truck sponsors it, and we donate ten percent of our proceeds."

"You cook here?"

"No. Our truck is parked outside. Didn't you see it? I don't know how you missed it! We have a subteam that works sometimes, and they take over on nights like this. DTF likes to be inside, supporting the women."

"DTF? Did I hear that right? *Down to fuck?*" I shook my head. The alcohol had clearly hit me. I crossed my fingers under the table, hoping I had heard her right.

"Dirty. Tough. Female. Not *down to fuck*, but ..." She scooted her chair closer to mine. "Repeat it in that accent of yours, and we will see."

"Oh." I fumbled my bottle down to the table, nearly spilling the few drops that were left. I needed those drops and preferably something even stronger.

I'd never had a woman come on to me so brazenly before. I would have to tell Aiden. He was right—both about the accent and about these women.

I discreetly leaned into the table, fanning out my elbows and mentally urging my pits to stop sweating before she noticed my wet pit stains growing. If my armpits could cry, this was what it would be like.

"I can tell you anything you'd like with my accent. Ever learned how to bathe a monkey?" I whispered into her ear.

"So, we selling the sauce to Crocodile Dundee over here or what?" Betty plopped herself down on a chair in front of us, interrupting the most play I'd had in years.

"What do you think? He said they'd buy it outright, and ten percent of proceeds from sales will have to go to the women's shelter. Isn't that right, Jay?" Rox ran her heel up the back of my calf under the table.

"Whatever you say. I mean … aye. Of course, we would do that! Scarlett Herb is all about giving back to the community." I jerked my head up and down, nodding at the both of them while shifting in my seat. My cock had thickened as soon as Rox scooted in closer to me.

"Moving on up, Rox. Don't put our Shizzle on some shit, Jay." Betty stood to go, narrowing her eyes down at me.

"Never." I pulled at my collar.

These Outer Forks women were going to be the death of me.

"About that monkey. I don't know how to bathe a monkey, but I've learned how you like to spank your monkey." She played with her empty beer bottle she'd nursed all night and inched even closer to me. Her thighs brushed against mine, making my cock leap up and my pants pitch a tent.

"I thought we weren't mentioning that ever again!"

"I liked it. I want to watch it again. You know, a walk of shame between our two houses isn't so bad, if you want a proper welcome to America. Southern hospitality and all." She shrugged her tiny bird-like shoulders. Her lips parted in a grin, begging for me to stick my dick between them.

"Let me get an Uber." I huffed, fumbling with my phone. I was out of breath like I'd jogged here from back home—Australia. I clutched my chest, not even sure I could breathe.

"Ride with me. Come to my place," she purred.

I could only blink and nod as she stood up and tugged my arm for me to follow her out.

We quickly made our exit, waving good-bye to the DTF group. They watched us like hawks as we left. I heard the ding from Rox's phone as soon as we settled into her car.

"Everything okay?" I asked.

"Yep. Let's go." She slammed her car door and sped off in the direction of our neighborhood.

FOUR

Rox

Betty: Are you sure?

Me: Yes.

Betty: You know the red flags.

Me: I know. He hasn't had any yet.

Betty: Yet.

I slid my phone back into my purse. Of course I wasn't going to pass up on a chance to bang this hot piece of wonder from Down Under. He had said all the right things to me and in that panty-melting accent. I couldn't resist. I glanced over at him as he buckled his seat belt and leaned back into the seat, fidgeting with his hands.

"Jay?" I asked.
"Yes?"

"You're okay with going back to my place, right? I can drop you off at yours, no problem, if you don't want to hang out. You look nervous."

"I am nervous. It's been a very long time for me. But I wouldn't turn down a chance with you for anything. I haven't stopped thinking about you since that night I saw you in the window. I'm drawn to you."

Draaawn. I bit my lip, and in my head, I tried to produce the sound he'd made.

"I'm drawn to you too. Not sure why. I'm used to the more rugged type, not pretentious—"

"Arsehats?" he asked.

Arse ...

"Right. You're not my type. No offense. I still find you hot as fuck and want to see your rocket blast off again. I'm just not used to the stuffy, straitlaced type with the button-down, sports jacket, styled hair, and clever tongue." I emphasized *clever tongue* in my best Aussie accent, failing miserably. It came out as a lisp—a bubbled, butchered lisp.

"So, you think just because I own a white-tableclothed restaurant, my attire is business casual, I'm well-groomed, and I speak the truth in my native tongue, that makes me not your type? Stuffy? Does that mean you think I can't get dirty?"

"Not as dirty as me. But let's get back to your native tongue. I like this tongue. I'd like to hear the way your Rs sound muffled between my thighs." I reached over and grabbed his cock as he let out a yelp. "See? I might be too wild for you. Maybe you can't handle me."

Without missing a beat, he cocked his head to the side and grinned, unzipping his pants and pulling himself out. I had seen it from a distance before and known already that it was almost so long that it could tickle the ceiling, but up close, it never ended.

Yes, please.

My tires squealed as I swerved my car to the left, narrowly missing the ditch.

"What are you doing? You can't whip your dick out and distract me when I'm driving! You're going to get us killed!"

I quickly glanced at him and put my eyes back on the road. His face was white with horror as he clutched his dick in his hand like it was the stick shift and he was trying to save us.

"Fuck! I was trying to be wild." He flinched, rubbing his strangled peter before gently tucking it back inside his pants.

I reached out, stopping his hand. "No. Keep it out. Keep playing. We're almost home," I said, turning into our neighborhood.

"All right," he growled. His hand went back to his cock, stroking it while he situated himself back into the seat. His other hand reached across for my thigh, pulling it toward him as he spread my legs.

I pulled into my driveway and slammed on the brakes, throwing my seat belt off in a ravenous fit.

It had been far too long for me also. The last few men I'd played with were months ago. They were friends with benefits, except their benefits expired the second they began falling for me. I'd felt nothing for them despite their efforts to win me over. Dead inside. That was me. After my ex-asshole-boyfriend, Tommy, I hadn't thought I could ever feel passion again.

But what I'd thought was a lost cause suddenly seemed to ignite in my loins again. Passionate, raw, hot, sweaty, dirty, animalistic desire flickered throughout my veins when Jay was around—and it wasn't just the sight of his explosive cock on steroids either that made me feel that way. Or his *come fuck me* accent. Or his rugged jawline. Or his piercing brown eyes. Or …

I crawled on top of him and pressed my mouth to his, straddling his lap and feeling his hardness between my thighs. His lips parted as I slipped my tongue in between them, teasing him. He tasted like something wild, something from the outback mixed with my favorite local beer. He grabbed my hips, rocking me back and forth over his cock.

"Let's take this inside," he muttered into my mouth.

I opened the car door and tumbled out, somersaulting like a ninja to save myself.

"I'm going to pretend that was a graceful ballerina move you just pulled to impress me." He quickly tucked himself back in his pants and pushed himself up and out of the car. "Are you all right?"

"Who says I'm trying to impress anyone? Maybe I just want to get laid." I pushed him into the side of my car, pinning myself against him and tipping my chin up for him to kiss me.

"I think you want more than that, sunshine," he whispered back to me, stroking my hair from my eyes.

I pushed myself off of him and took a step back, swallowing hard. "What makes you say that? You don't even know me," I scoffed, feeling too vulnerable for comfort.

"Wishful thinking. Sorry. Sometimes, I say things before I think them through. I feel like I do know you, oddly enough. There's this connection between us. I've never felt this way before. Is that weird? Do you feel that too? I lose my breath at the thought of you. I blow my load at the sight of you! I swear that's not happened before—ever."

"I feel it," I sighed. "It's a magnetism, a comfort, security, passion, lust. It's all those good things. But it's sex. Just sex. That's what you're after, right?"

"No. Not at all. I want a partner. I mean, don't get me wrong; I want sex too. But I'd prefer the type of sex on the regular—with someone I can get to know. Someone I like, and I like you, Rox."

He shrugged his shoulders and looked up toward the sky. The moonlight shone down on his face, highlighting his tightened jawline. I watched the dip in his jaw as he clenched and unclenched his teeth.

"Call it fate, call it divine intervention, call it what you will. But here we are, and I think, maybe in another life or something, we knew each other. I don't know how else to explain it. I know you. It's not just sex for me, but if that is more comforting for you, then that is what it will be."

"What did you say? Divine intervention? You believe in all of that stuff?"

"I know it," he said, still staring up into space.

I sighed and looked up at the stars too. Divine intervention all right. Someone up there was cockblocking me with these feelings shit. But he was right; I felt it. The second he'd stepped from around The Pink Taco Truck and into view, I'd lost my breath. I couldn't explain it. Maybe it was the damn crystals hanging all over the truck.

What is this shit? Why do I feel so … close to him? Why does he feel so … close to me? It's because he doesn't know me. Once he gets to know me, he will run far, far away, back to Australia.

"Let's keep it just sex. You don't want me." I shook my head and turned my gaze back to him.

I couldn't be what he needed—a partner, as he'd called it. The only type who would be able to handle me and my scars was someone a lot more rugged than this prim-and-proper sex god standing before me.

"I'm looking at you right now, and I can tell you, as a matter of fact, I do want you. And I have since I spotted you in the window. It's no coincidence we've kept bumping into each other. I think we were meant to date. But why would you think I don't want you? I've not given you that impression, I hope."

"I'm trouble. I've been through a lot," I mumbled, scuffing the toe of my shoe across the pavement. "I'm not sure I would even know how to be in a normal relationship. I'm broken. You don't want this. Trust me."

Points to myself for playing it safe. Boundaries!

I mentally patted myself on the back even though what I wanted to do was punch myself in the face.

"You're not broken," he whispered, stepping in front of me. He reached out to me, putting his finger under my chin and gently lifting my gaze to meet his. "You're *kintsugi.*"

"What did you just call me? Is that some kind of Japanese train wreck? I don't know who she is."

I pulled my brows together and tried to look at him fiercely, but his gaze made me melt. I was putty in his hands—or a puddle. He would need to mop me up because even as a Japanese train wreck, I became soaking wet.

"She's you. *Kintsugi* is the Japanese art form of taking broken pieces and melding them back together again with gold. Your scars, your broken pieces. They're golden and only make you more beautiful."

This man ... is not even from this earth.

I gulped back a silent sob and turned my attention back to the stars above me. My eyes blinked rapidly as they pushed those pesky tears back into their hiding place. For once in my life, I was speechless. This had never happened before. We stood there in silence for a long moment, but it wasn't awkward. It was peaceful.

I cleared my throat. "No one has ever said anything like that to me. Where did you even get that from?"

He cocked his head to the side and grinned. "From my head. It's what I see when I look at you. I also see the most gorgeous woman I've ever laid eyes on. She's clever, funny, witty, strong, motivated, and a total badass. She's *kintsugi*. You're *kintsugi*. I don't care about your brokenness. All I see is gold."

I curled my fingers around his belt loops and pulled his hips into mine. I could feel his never-ending cock, thick and restless as a snake moving around in his pants. "Let's go. Now," I whispered, peeling myself off of him and tugging him toward my door.

He followed behind me, his hand gripping mine so hard that our knuckles turned white. We barely made it in the door before he picked me up and threw me over his shoulder, turning his cheek to bite me on my ass—*arse*—hard.

I closed my eyes and groaned. "Upstairs, first room on the left," I huffed, running my hands down the back of his pants and sliding them up and over his firm butt.

I bounced against him with each quick step he took toward my bedroom. Each bounce I felt vibrated throughout my entire body, sending tingles from my toes to my scalp. My whole body came alive, throbbing, needing, aching for him to take it. All of it. I would be his broken Japanese pottery tonight.

"Um." He stood at the bottom of the stairs, pausing briefly.

I patted his buns. "Giddy up! What are ya waiting on?"

"There's no railing. I don't want to drop you or hurt you."

"Oh. You can do it! I bet you wrestle gators over there. Besides, you can't hurt me. I kinda like a little bit of pain."

With one quick movement, he slid me down into the cradle of his arms, my face inches from his.

"I'll not hurt you. I feel much better, holding you like this. Now, I get to see that gorgeous face of yours. Not that I didn't mind the arse." He grinned, gave me a peck on the lips, and hurled us forward.

"You know, Jay, I'm impressed. Here you are, carrying me around, and you're still not out of breath."

"Stamina. It's my thing." He reached the top of the stairs, still holding me securely in his arms.

"Oh?"

"You'll see."

"Oh." I blushed. I never blushed.

What is this man doing to me? It's the accent. Has to be the accent.

My heart began to beat faster as he took one … two … three … steps to my door and peered inside. I reached out to the side and flicked a light switch on, my eyes not leaving his. I watched the reflection of my prim-and-proper bedroom in his pupils as they adjusted.

"Wow. It looks like a five-star hotel here. I wouldn't have guessed—"

"What would you have guessed?" I smiled sweetly up at him. "Something more dark and moody? A dungeon maybe?"

"Exactly. Or a witch's lair." He lay me down atop my plush feathered comforter.

"Ha-ha-ha-ha! Here we go with that lunch-lady-slash-witch theory again." I cackled, crawling to my nightstand and opening the drawer. "Hair of dog and eye of newt, wrap your dick if you want this coot!" I tossed him a condom.

His lips smashed together in a thin line, twitching. "Bewitching woman, poisoned brew, I'll do as you say and not give you the Australian fuck flu."

"That was good! See there? You're a poet and didn't know it!" I nodded, lifting my dress up and over my head and throwing it to the side. I sat, completely naked and completely comfortable, sinking into my feathered bed as he took me in with his eyes.

"Oi, oi, oi!" His eyes bulged as he licked his lips.

I noticed a tiny vein right below the hairline on his left temple pulsating. I wondered if it matched the pulsing of his thick, veined cock.

"Come on over here, and fark me, mate. I'll not cast any spells on yar," I said in a weird mixture of Australian and pirate accent.

"You already have," he sighed, crawling on top of me.

I fumbled with the buttons on his stiff, starched shirt, exposing a set of abs that I had only seen in movies. He rendered me speechless again but only for a moment.

Blushing and speechless? I think it's him who is casting a spell.

"I had no idea you were hiding that under your suit and ties! You should be wearing ... nothing. Just walk around with your shirt off. You'd probably be even busier at your restaurant. Actually, you could wear a bow tie. One of those stripper ones. That's it," I rambled on as he slipped his pants and boxers off and neatly set them on the edge of the bed.

He had the V-cut. That ridge of muscle that went from hip bone to heaven. I wanted to trace it with my tongue.

"Is that what you like?" He sat upon his knees, rolling the rubber onto his dick. "Tell me what you like," he growled, leaning back over me.

"You. I like you," I breathed out before I had any sense to stop myself.

That was one way to get a man to run. Especially on a first night's fling. Not that I minded at this point. I kind of wanted to run myself. Sex I could do, but whatever bumbling mess this man made me wasn't what I'd expected.

He reached below my navel, running his finger up and down my slit before pushing it inside me. I wrapped my legs around his back and pulled him in closer, bucking my needy hips.

"Show me," I whispered. My lips grazed the side of his cheek before I took his earlobe between my teeth and hissed in his ear, "Show me what *you* like."

He grabbed my wrists and pinned them down up over my head while expertly guiding himself into me. So. Fucking. Slow.

I closed my eyes and concentrated on feeling every single inch of him. His dick didn't quit. I thought if he kept going, he would see the tip pop out of my mouth and wink at him.

Just how much of him is in there? Fuck! How long is this thing?

I squirmed against him, needing him to do me fast and hard, like I was used to being done. I'd never had slow sex before, and it wasn't that I wasn't enjoying it. Believe me, I was loving it. Too much. As in … my heart was getting into this shit. This wasn't just my vag and his cock playing peekaboo. This was my whole body on fire and alive because he was fucking every single inch of my soul.

I made the mistake of fluttering my eyes open and meeting his gaze. The smile that played over his lips made my breath catch in my throat as I tried to moan out the emotions bubbling up inside of me. The same ones I had kept hidden deep down into the crevices—or cracks … golden cracks—where they belonged.

He pushed his lips against mine, and I *felt* him still smiling. I said good-bye to my brain and let my body operate on autopilot, responding to his touch like it had never been touched before. Like I hadn't just touched it this morning—twice and while watching some wild new clip from the porn king Malcolm Beaumont's website.

Waves, quivers, and puppy-dog eyes—*puppy-dog eyes?*—snuck up on me, betraying my tough-cookie exterior and turning me into a puddle of goo in his gator-wrestling Australian hands. I shut my eyes tight, trying to think of something to stop the emotions surfacing right under my skin.

Take control. I need to take control.

I raised my neck up and roughly pressed my lips back into his. The stubble on his chin scratched against my cheeks, causing them to redden. It was that—not him. Not me. I wasn't blushing again.

"Yes, please." He grinned.

His sparkly, perfect smile widened as I pushed him over and straddled myself on top. Pinning his wrists over his head, I started to grind.

At first, I thought my eyes were playing tricks on me, so I closed them again and kept slamming myself against him. But when I opened them next, I realized I hadn't been seeing things. Jay's eyes really were crossed—and not slightly crossed. He had crossed them to the point where I only saw mostly the whites of his eyeballs. I slowed down and freaked the fuck out. His eyes jolted back into their proper place.

"Something wrong?" he asked as I sat back, still rocking.

"Nope. Nothing. Not at all. Just wondering if this is okay for you. I don't want to scare you with hard-core sex instead of all that touchy-feely, slow stuff," I answered, quickening my pace.

"You liked the slow stuff." He smirked.

"I like all the stuff."

I ran my palms up his rock-hard chest, feeling every ripple, every curve, and every heartbeat. I quickly pulled them back as if I'd touched a hot stove.

No hearts. Just cock and balls, I told myself.

I clenched my thighs around him tight and bounced harder as his hands grasped my hips and held on for dear life. His eyes grew wider and wider, following the bouncing of my small breasts. I moaned louder, speeding myself up even more. If I rubbed against him any faster, I'd probably set us both on fire. My toes began to tingle, signaling my body that I was on edge and about to tip over.

"I'm so close. Are you ready?" I moaned between breaths. I hadn't worked this hard in a long time. Already, I felt spent.

"I can keep going, but if you're ready, I'm ready."

I nodded, remembering the load he had shot off when I watched him playing with himself through the window. I'd never seen a man blow his load so forcefully and dramatically. I wondered if he was going to burst forth through that condom and shoot me off him like a rocket ship.

"Say when," he growled.

Really? What black magic fuckery is this? Say when? That's it?

"When," I managed to squeak out before my body started to convulse.

My thighs shook as I clenched down hard on him and moaned loud enough to echo off my walls. His eyes immediately did the spooky crossy thing as he pushed himself into me so deep that my eyes also did the spooky crossy thing. I swore I felt the tip of him tickling the back of my throat. Did I mention that his dick didn't quit?

"Fark! Oi!" he cried out as I nervously bit my lip and bore down, hoping the condom stayed put with his dick hydrant.

I slowed my pace, finally stopping, and hopped off my ride.

Phew.

The rubber was still in place and stuffed like a water balloon.

"Um"—I pointed at the time bomb that was his wrapped cock—"that's about to explode."

"Right!" He hopped up. "Bathroom?"

I pointed toward the bathroom door and watched his tight apple booty walk away. My body still throbbed, my clit pulsing. I smiled to myself, knowing I'd feel this tomorrow. That was my favorite part of wild, crazy sex—being sore enough to remember it the day after. I pulled the covers back and snuggled myself inside, cozy and satisfied.

"That was on the verge of being messy!" He sauntered back into the room, sliding into bed next to me. "You know there's no Australian fuck flu, right? And as embarrassing as this is, I'd not slept with anyone in two years. I'm clean. But I understand if you're not on birth control."

"I am on birth control actually. But how can I trust you're not lying to me? I don't trust just any man who tells me he is clean."

"I'm not asking you to trust me. I'd not push you into anything." He leaned down to kiss me. "I'm just letting you know that I'm not some playboy. If you want to trust me, you will. In time."

"Thanks. Are you saying you want another time in my witch's lair? I didn't scare you away?"

He pulled the covers back, tracing his index finger along my collarbone and grinning.

"Is that what that was? You trying to scare me away? Well, you can't scare me. I ... liked it. I've never had a woman be so ... ballsy for my ballsies." He laughed.

"Really? I don't know how you keep them from ravishing you!"

"I'd not had many chances. I've only been in two serious relationships, and for the last few years, I've been too busy traveling the world."

"Wow. I've never been outside of the US! Where was your favorite place? I'd love to visit Paris one day!" I settled into his arms, ready for story time.

"Easy. It was Rome. I've never traveled anywhere I didn't enjoy, but Rome is magical. The food, the people, the atmosphere—it's very fairy tale. Old world. For an old soul like me, I suppose."

He continued tracing over my collarbone, working his way down to my tattoos. His eyes crinkled as he studied them, reading me like a book. I flushed hot, knowing what was coming next. They always asked.

"Now, you tell me something. These tattoos, what do they mean?"

"What do you mean, what do they mean? Why do they have to mean anything?"

"I don't know. Don't people usually get tattoos that have some type of significant meaning to them? Like, this one, what were you saying when you got it?" He gently tapped the bluebird on my collar.

"It doesn't mean anything. It just looked cool, so I got it." All of the tension that had left my body earlier was now back threefold.

"Really? So, you only get tattoos that look cool? Nothing significant, aye?"

"Okay. Maybe a few are significant," I sighed. "Are you trying to be scared away again?"

"Like I said, you can't scare me. My life hasn't been picture-perfect either."

I hesitated before I turned away from him, lifting my hair and rolling over to show him my latest tattoo. I had gone straight to the tattoo parlor with Betty the day after I found the courage to leave Tommy.

"This one. On the back of my neck. Closest to my brain, so I don't make another dumb mistake. Check it out."

I heard a sudden, sharp intake of breath as he ran his fingertips over my raven.

"What's a matter? You think ravens are creepy? You know, they are super-smart birds," I said to an awkward silence. "Did I finally scare you away?" I turned my head to make sure he hadn't disappeared.

He hadn't said a word, and I was beginning to second-guess that I really did have a raven on the nape of my hairline and not something crazy, like a gerbil or a banana.

"It's beautiful," he said, moving in closer to me. His breath tickled my ear, sending a vibration down my body. "So, what does your raven mean?"

"Nevermore," I whispered.

He put his palm on my shoulder, turning me to meet his eyes. He didn't ask questions, and he didn't make jokes. Instead, he held me there, tight, in the moment. My body began to wake again as he pulled the covers from atop me and swept his gaze up and down my very exposed and very vulnerable being.

"*Kintsugi*," he whispered, brushing his lips against mine and crawling on top of me.

I gave in, letting out a breath I'd held on for far too long. I let him fuck me slowly.

FIVE

Jay

I hadn't meant to fall asleep at Rox's house, but between her feathered bed and her soft breaths, I'd been lulled into sleeping like the dead. I hadn't woken up once in the middle of the night, whereas at my house, I woke every hour on the hour.

The filtered sunlight peeking through the blinds woke me up from my deep sleep. I rubbed my eyes and crept as quietly as I could out of bed, slipping on my pants.

"Mmm," Rox sighed from beneath the covers.

I glanced over at her small frame, lost in the mountain of pillows and blankets. For an inked-up badass, at that moment, she looked as tiny and frail as a bird—a raven. Tough as nails but still fragile.

"Jay?" she called, reaching out beside her to an empty bed.

"Shh. Go back to sleep. I've got to do my morning run. I'll text you later." I smoothed her hair back from her face and smiled.

"Okay. You don't have to ask me to sleep. On it." She pulled the covers up to her chin and, oddly enough, fell right back to sleep. Immediately.

Her breaths deepened, and her nose whistled out a tune that sent me into silent giggles. I shook my head and tiptoed out of her room.

I snuck out the side door, making sure I locked it behind me, and headed home to dress in my running gear. I needed to clear my head of everything that had happened last night. Every. Wonderful. Thing. And what it meant.

Did it mean anything? The raven tattoo?

My hair stood on end as I shivered, rubbing the back of my neck.

Last night had felt good—too good. Rox fit perfectly into my arms throughout the night. Her body melted into mine, and all I could think about before we drifted off to sleep was when she told me she didn't want to make a dumb mistake again. She never explained her situation, but I slowly began to put the pieces together between some of our conversations and her work at the women's shelter. I had pulled her in tight to me right before my eyes shut for the night. I wanted to wrap her up and keep her safe.

I greeted the damp morning air with a grimace. It was April and yet still chilly outside until about mid-morning. The weather back home wasn't anything like this. I preferred the familiar Australian heat to the dewy, cold mist of Outer Forks. The spring chill was for the birds.

Birds.

The birds chirped in the trees as the sun began to rise behind the park. I expected and hoped for a full-on morning serenade as I ran through the hills. I never ran with headphones in and music blaring. I preferred silence or the sounds of the forest. I listened intently to my surroundings. Maybe, with this peaceful morning, my brain would clear enough to show some clarity on my new life and if I was headed in the right direction—which I hoped was settling down for good. I perked my ears as I entered the park. Maybe the call of a raven would lead me to where I needed to go.

I quickened my pace and bolted off through the trails.

I made it into work before the brunch rush. The smell of freshly squeezed orange juice and champagne instantly energized my spent body. Last night, I'd blown the life force out of me three times, and this morning, I'd hit the pavement with complete mental exhaustion. I felt sluggish, rolling into work, but the energy of Scarlett Herb zapped me back on my toes.

I headed toward the kitchen and opened the swinging doors to the chaos that was brunch. This type of wild was the only chaos I liked, and even I couldn't take too much of it. My pace had always been slow and steady in the background. Throwing me into the mess would be even crazier, but my consulting and management skills seemed to calm the most hectic of days for everyone.

I had heard that compliment often—that I was a calm presence. My demeanor was kind, gentle, empathetic, and peaceful. I was happy enough with those compliments, but I also wished I had heard I rocked between the sheets or I was toe-curling or something more attractive than *nice*.

"Morning, Jay!" My brother shoved an apron in my hand. "Prep work. We're shorthanded today. It's all you! Start chopping."

He snapped his fingers together and danced around. I wondered if he'd gotten laid last night too.

"Great. Because I'd love to stand on my feet some more after that run in the woods earlier." I sighed.

I tied the apron around my waist, washed my hands, and began to work. The fast-paced action helped the morning pass by quicker than anticipated. By the time I finished dicing eighty-two thousand onions, my eyes were swollen red and on fire. I rubbed them, like a dumbass, and made the pain even worse.

"Back in a moment," I squealed at the team as I stumbled my way to the restroom. I could barely see my way around with my stinging, watery eyes.

"Jay! Just who I wanted to see," a familiar voice called from behind me.

I squinted and turned to see Betty standing in the corridor, her hands crossed over her chest. There was something in the way she smiled that made me think it was more of a snarl or a warning. My butt involuntarily clenched.

"Oh, hey! Betty. How are you? Are you here for brunch?" I asked.

"Have you been crying? Wow, she really must have done a number on you last night. Maybe I don't need to have this talk with you after all." Betty stepped closer to me, putting her hands on my shoulders and searching my face.

I looked at her through the swollen slits of my eyes and shook my head. "What? No! I've not been crying. I was chopping onions. What do you mean, a talk? Rox did something? I'm confused." I pressed the heel of my palms to my eyes, hoping that would make the stinging go away.

"You don't have goggles? We have some in the truck. I'll grab them. Stay there. Or … go rinse your eyes or something. I'll be right back. Don't go hiding either. I still need to have a word with you. We all do."

"All?"

"Think DTF doesn't travel in packs? Boy, bye. Be right back!"

I splashed cold water on my eyes and studied myself in the mirror. I couldn't believe she'd thought I had been crying. Not that I had a hard time crying. Those damn Hallmark movies got me every time.

What did she mean by saying Rox did a number on me?

I leaned into the sink and hung my head, not yet ready to find out what kind of conversation waited for me on the other side of the door.

Betty cracked the restroom door open and yelled inside, "What in the hell are you doing in there? Come on out here. We got business to handle!"

I yelped and made my exit.

"Took long enough."

"My eyes were on fire! I had to fix them," I whispered in a shaky voice.

We stood, pushing ourselves against the wall in the narrow hallway as a few customers filed in and out of the restrooms.

"Here." She handed me a pair of goggles. "It's for cutting onions. You're welcome."

"That's genius. Thanks. I appreciate it." I pressed my lips together and nodded, reaching out for them before she snatched her hand back.

"But first, Rox. I'm assuming y'all hooked up last night?"

Betty narrowed her eyes at me, and I instantly felt my balls tighten. Her fierce expression that played across her face cracked a whip, like a rubber band popping me in the nuts.

"Well, I'm not sure what kind of men are around here, but I'm a gentleman, and I don't kiss and tell." I lowered my voice as yet another customer squeezed past us.

"Cut the shit. I know Rox. She looked at you like she wanted to eat you up. Whatever you told her worked. I'm just here to tell you, watch it. I don't know if you know any of this, but she's been healing from a terrible relationship."

"Nevermore," I muttered, my heart dropping into my stomach.

"She told you?"

"Well, no. Not really. She showed me her raven tattoo but didn't elaborate. I'm smart enough not to push her into explaining. I assumed she had been through some bad shit. Especially considering how much she is invested into the shelter and all."

"You ain't lying. Rox has been through hell, and DTF won't let her do it again. Understood? So, if you come up over here, talking all that sexy, wet-panty Crocodile Dundee talk, and then hurt her, I will cut you up and serve your ass on a taco. New taco on our menu. He Should Have Stayed in Oz taco. Extra salty."

I glanced down the hall toward the exit. My balls had shriveled up so far into my body that I was sure they were hiding in my throat, making it hard for me to swallow. This was the exact reason I had played it safe with the bubbly women who wouldn't dare hurt a fly—except Elena. She had broken my heart in two. I couldn't win for losing. Maybe I'd had it all wrong.

"I am not that type of man. I like Rox. A lot. I would never hurt her or anyone. I think, if anything, she might be the one to hurt me. She tried pushing me away several times last night." I noticed Betty's fists clench. "Not physically!" I continued. "Definitely not physically, but mentally. She kept going on and on about how I wouldn't want her or she might scare me away. But I do want her. It's the oddest thing ever. I'm terrified of her yet enthralled by her. I feel ... connected to her somehow."

"It's the crystals." Nikki popped up behind me, shaking a crystal that hung around her neck. "I've been using them more often, and we have them all over the truck. Rox even grabbed one, although she grabbed orange carnelian, which is good for sex. I'm guessing it worked since we are all here today, as per Betty's orders."

"It worked! I can see it in his eyes. He has been crying. He feels so strongly about her!" Layla piped in.

Betty rolled her eyes and said, "Layla, he's been cutting onions," before turning back to me and lowering her voice. "Don't hurt her. She's fragile."

"Like a bird." I nodded, meeting her eyes.

"Like a bomb," Nikki said, twirling her crystal necklace around her finger and staring me down.

"I think he's got the point, ladies. Let's make some Shizzle! Point us to the kitchen Jay man! I didn't mean to scare you!" Betty put her arms around me, bringing me in for a hug. "I'll skin your Crocodile Dundee ass into a new alligator handbag. Don't you forget it," she whispered before letting me go and smiling.

I tried to smile back, but all I could manage was a whimper.

"Jay?" Aiden stuck his head out of the kitchen doors. "You okay? We need you in here."

I wanted to mouth, *Help*, but instead, I introduced him to our new business partners.

"How can we help?" Layla walked over to Aiden and adjusted her V-neck sweater that clung to her well-rounded chest.

"Right this way." Aiden stepped aside and held the door open for DTF. His eyes hadn't left Layla. They followed her, lingering on her hips as she sauntered past him.

"So, this is Scarlett Herb. Y'all must cook with a lot of saffron to name it after a red herb!" Layla tilted her head to Aiden.

"Actually, no. Scarlett was my mother's name, and Herb was my father." Aiden nodded, still smiling. "Welcome to my dungeon, ladies. I'll show you the ropes, and you can make your Shizzle Sauce. Just be warned: you came at brunch rush. It could get a bit chaotic in here!"

"Oh, Aiden. We are the chaos." Nikki shook her head and grabbed an apron.

"We'll be on our best behavior. Your boy Terrance hooked us up with some of them fancy mimosas. I'd say we are all feeling fine, and we'll be one big, happy family after today." Betty caught my eye and winked.

Aiden's eyebrows rose as he looked back and forth from me to Betty. We locked eyes for a second, but in that second, we communicated silently that we might have just gotten ourselves in over our heads. No, we had definitely gotten ourselves in over our heads. For *Shizzle*.

By the time DTF left, the brunch rush had quieted, and business lulled to a slow and steady pace. I could barely keep my eyes open after the chaotic morning and the non-restful night. I ducked out of the kitchen, letting Aiden know I needed a catnap and would be back shortly. I left out the part that it was because I'd stayed up all night, having a sexathon with Rox, who had worn my ass out. I had planned on being gentle and slow with her, but she'd had other plans. Not that I had anything to complain about. I liked the wild ride.

I arrived back home in record time and made my way up to the guest room. I still hadn't fully unpacked my master bedroom, and at this point, I didn't care. With views straight across the way of that beautiful, inked goddess, I didn't want to move. I stood at the window and lifted the blinds, quickly peeking out before I lay down to nap. I gasped and did a double-take into Rox's backyard. She stood, bent over in her flowerbed, completely naked, except for a floppy sunhat. I watched her back muscles flex in the sunlight as she pulled weed after weed. My cock stirred, lengthening in my pants.

"Fuck," I breathed out.

Our homes were the last ones on the street, next to the park and trails, thankfully. No one else had this view but me. Even then, I admired her bravery and confidence to put herself on display. That was something I could never do, but it must feel so … freeing.

I pulled out my phone, texting her before realizing she had nowhere to store her phone and she wouldn't see it.

> *Me: Hey there. What's a gorgeous woman like you doing all that dirty work for? And naked? Is this an American custom I don't know about?*

I watched through my blinds as she rose up and walked back to her patio, picking up the phone from the edge of a chair. She glanced up to see me in the window, shook her tits, and waved.

> *Rox: Happy World Naked Gardening Day! If you couldn't already tell, I like it dirty.*

> *Me: And fast.*

I leaned into the window. I couldn't pull my eyes away from her. The way the sunlight sparkled on her shimmering skin sent tingles shooting up the base of my cock. I was on the verge of erupting again already.

> *Rox: Do I ever! I love going fast. Spinning out of control. It's my thing. I need the momentum to keep going.*

> *Me: So, that's what happened last night? That was you going fast to keep going. I liked it. I also love taking things slow, so I can feel every vibration your body makes when I'm diving deep inside of you.*

Rox brushed the dirt off of her legs and sat on the edge of her chair before answering me.

> *Rox: Wow! You have a way with words. You're a rock star, do you know that? Thanks for last*

night. I needed it. Fast, slow. It was perfect. You're amazing. I've got to finish these weeds before it rains. Storms are coming this afternoon and sticking around the rest of the week. Talk soon.

I still peered down at her as she set the phone down and went back to digging in the dirt. She moved delicately, almost floating across her yard. I wondered how someone could be so tough yet so graceful. My phone buzzed in my pocket, pulling me out of my trance. Aiden's name flashed across the screen.

"We need you. We just booked a party of fifteen for tonight. Can you drink some coffee and come back now?" he said as soon as I answered the phone.

"Sure, sure," I sighed, shutting my blinds and heading back out.

I apologized to my dick and promised it shenanigans later.

It had been three days since I last saw Rox. I kept checking my phone to see if she'd texted, but I was only met with nothing. She hadn't reached out to me after that naked-gardening incident even though I'd texted her to let her know our Shizzle dish was going well. She responded in short texts and emojis only. I backed off, not wanting to scare her away this time. But I couldn't stop thinking of her and the night we'd shared. She had set up residence in my brain. She remained there since that evening at her place, a constant, warm ember lighting my body, mind, and soul. I felt more alive with her than I had felt even after traveling the entire world.

"This is stupid," I muttered to myself.

I checked the time on my phone. It was a little after midnight. I tossed and turned and couldn't get myself to sleep. Not even spanking my monkey had helped tonight. I pulled myself up from the bed and tied a robe around my waist, pacing the floor. I knew what had been keeping me up tonight. It was her—or the lack thereof. I hadn't heard Rox's car door slam shut yet. She wasn't home, and it was getting late.

My mind raced with the possibilities of her being hurt or in need of help or even in bed with another man. The hair on the back of my neck bristled. I debated on if I should check in on her or not but figured that would be not only creepy, but she might think I was nosy too.

But what if there was an accident?

I made myself a cup of tea and rummaged through my box of books that I hadn't yet unpacked. I settled on a historical novel that Elena had left behind—*Memphis Queen* by Christopher Kaiser. I would read anything to get my mind off my bird not returning to her nest.

I made myself comfy, sitting up in bed, and thumbed through the pages when I heard it. That familiar slam of her car door released tension in me that I hadn't realized I was holding on to. My shoulders dropped, my chest dropped, and my blood pressure dropped. I breathed a sigh of relief and continued reading. Rox was home safe, and all was well in the world. My phone buzzed beside me.

What the fuck?

Roxie's name flashed across the screen.

"Hello? Roxie, you okay?" I answered.

"Are you? Your light is on! You're never up this late, Gramps. Why are you up? Are you sick or something?" Rox's tone caught me off guard. She sounded as worried as I had been moments earlier.

"No. I just couldn't sleep. How come you are up so late?"

"Long night at the shelter. We had a new lady come in with two little girls. It was rough." Her voice dropped low, barely above a whisper.

"Want to talk about it?"

"No."

"Okay. You're such a hard worker. I want you to know that I think you're amazing for all the things you do. You seem to take care of everyone though. Do you ever do anything for yourself?"

"Like what? I write poetry. You know that. That's kind of for myself, I guess."

"That's great! I think you need to do some more stuff, too, though—something just for you. You deserve to with all you've got going on. Also, I've been thinking, and I'd like to do something just for you, too, if you'll let me. You work too hard. You should be taken care of as well." I listened to her sigh softly into the phone.

"I do take care of everyone, but I don't need any help or anyone to take care of me."

I took a long sip of my tea and contemplated my next move. "I know you don't need anyone to take care of you, but would you let someone if they wanted to?"

"Depends. What would I owe them?"

"Nothing. Why would you owe anyone anything?"

"That's just how it usually works. I feel like I owe them, or they usually expect me to owe them."

"Not for me. That isn't how it is supposed to work, but if that makes you feel better, then how about this? We can make a pact or a treaty or whatever you want to call it. I pick three things I think you'd enjoy, and you pick three things you think I'd enjoy, and let's do those things for each other. Will that make you feel better about me doing something for you?"

"I get to pick three things for you to do?" Her voice lifted.

"Yes, or we can do three things for each other. Just something for us—and only us."

"No DTF, eh? Sorry about them bombarding you. I heard all about it. Betty is just protective."

"As well as a good friend should be. No worries."

"So, this treaty, does it have any rules?"

"Nope. As much as that makes my arse clench to think of what you could come up with when I say no rules, there aren't any. The only rule we have is, no backing out. Does that sound fair to you?"

My mind raced. Roxie would have me jumping out of a plane this weekend; I knew it.

"I like this idea. I'll have my list for you tomorrow. I'm down for whatever. I don't think there is anything you could throw at me that would scare me, so let's do it. You, on the other hand, be afraid. Be very, very, afraid." She gave a maniacal laugh.

"I've been in your witch's lair. You can't scare me away either."

"Good. I don't want to," she whispered.

I smiled and reached over to turn off my light.

"Rox, can I sing to you? A lullaby. I know you've had a rough day. I want to send you off with the best of dreams."

"Really? You want to sing? To me? Okay. Sure. I've never had anyone sing to me before or care about my rough days." Her voice trailed off.

I scooted down into the covers and cleared my throat.

"Well, times are a-changing. Ready?" I asked.

"Do it."

I sang "Blackbird" by The Beatles into the phone like I was on Broadway. My voice hit notes that I'd made when I was kicked in the nuts in high school. I even nailed that really high part about flying into the night. I finished off strong, ready to stand up in bed and give myself an ovation, but the silence from the other end made my heart plummet into my stomach.

"Rox? Are you still there? Did I scare you away?" My voice shook. I worried my song choice hit too close to home with the broken wings reference.

"That was beautiful," she whispered.

I heard the smile in her voice and let out my breath. I'd fucking scored. I pictured her in the window, holding up a ten scorecard.

"Thank you. You're beautiful. Sleep well, sunshine."

"Sleep well, rock star Jay."

I hung up the phone and fell asleep, smiling.

I awoke the next morning, refreshed and ready to take on whatever life could throw at me. I had a beautiful raven next door to me, a job I loved, a new home full of possibilities, and a fresh start at life. I'd left my baggage in Australia, and now, nothing could bring me down. Nothing.

The sun shone through my window as I eased myself out of bed and shuffled toward the closet. I slipped my running gear on and headed toward the door. Even the sight of her window and knowing she was in her home, still fast asleep, zapped excited energy into me. I jogged past her house and hit the trails, thinking of a list of fun things for Rox. I had endless ideas, but I needed to make sure these things were new to her. I wanted to sweep her off her feet and soar through happy experiences with her.

I thought about reaching out to DTF but remembered we'd said this treaty would be between us only. I couldn't break my vow. I wouldn't even ask Aiden for help. True to my word, I would do this on my own—for her. Something told me she needed it, and I thought I did too.

My feet hit the ground hard, and my abs tightened. The endorphins coursed through my body, brain, heart.

My runner's high lasted the entire run and even for a while after I finished. I returned home with a pep in my step.

I danced toward the shower, turning it on as hot as it could go to knock the chilly morning off of me. A cold shiver tickled up my spine, but the sunshine next door had kept my brain on fire. I stepped into the steam, letting the water stream over my face, my smile, my cock. I reached down to give it a few tugs—you know, to clear my mind even more. I had an important task to finish. I needed the clarity that came with an empty mind and an empty ballsack.

I shot my load all over the place while I imagined the way Rox had looked, bouncing on me. Her perfectly perky breasts moving in sync with her hips ... up and down and up and down. The way she'd looked at me when I slowly drove myself into her. I needed that again, ached for it. Her blue eyes had practically begged for it, and I wanted to give it all to her. Everything.

I knew, without a doubt, one of my assignments in the treaty would be a date. Maybe I could have a taste of her again then. For a fleeting moment, I thought about writing *butt sex* into the treaty but only for a moment. I still considered myself a gentleman. Butt sex could come later.

I stepped out of the shower and dried myself off, flexing my pecs in the mirror. I shook my hips in a little happy dance and hummed love songs. Today would be spectacular. I would make it so. Maybe I would even stop by her taco truck for lunch—with flowers. I was going to get a dozen smiles from her because pleasing her was pleasing me—win-win. Endorphins kept pumping through my veins as my brain raced with sappy scenarios.

My phone vibrated on the nightstand, interrupting my train of thought. I rolled my eyes, thinking Aiden wanted me to pick up something before work—probably more avocados. Hipsters loved those things.

I picked my phone up and read a text from Rox.

Rox: Treaty of Treat Yo'self

I hereby declare Jaxon Taylor to go to Westy's, the amusement park, with me this weekend, to get a tattoo, and to write a poem.

Signed,

Your Partner in Crime

Fuck.

I read her text eight times, slowly, making sure I was reading it right and cursing myself for the no-rules rule. She wanted me to go fast, mark myself permanently, and share my feelings. I was utterly fucked—and not in the way I wanted to be either.

SIX

Rox

My work at the women's shelter left me mentally and physically exhausted. Between caring for the women and children there and our taco truck business, I had become a walking zombie—albeit a happy, smitten, and banking zombie. The Shizzle Sauce had taken off at Scarlett Herb, and by the end of the week, they had already needed more. Layla and Betty had been quick to volunteer to make the sauce over the weekend. Nikki had said something about a hot bartender for Betty, and Layla had her eyes on Aiden.

When it rained, it poured. For a group of women who had been single for so long, men were beginning to rain down on us.

Nikki had had her date with the cute officer, and she said he hadn't even put any moves on her and barely spoken a word. She didn't like shy men. She needed loud, wild, and reckless guys to match her personality. Nikki had always been the daring one, trying new things. Lately, she had been starring at amateur night at the local strip club,

The Steamy Clam. She'd brought in four hundred bucks just from that one night. We had told her it was her amazing talent, but she blamed the crystals—always the crystals.

And as much as I didn't believe in all the voodoo magic, there was no other explanation for the way I felt about Jay. He had come out of nowhere and blindsided me. Everything about him felt familiar. He was comfortable, peaceful, gentle—polar opposite of what I was used to dating.

"He called me kintsugi," I told DTF one morning during prep.

"The fuck? I will kill him! You aren't a kintsugi! What the hell is a kintsugi?" Betty slapped her spatula on the countertop.

Layla and Nikki had stopped in their tracks, also posed to kill with their kitchen utensils.

"No, no. It's a good thing. I told him I was broken and flawed, and he told me that I wasn't broken. I am kintsugi. It's the Japanese art form where the artist melds together broken pieces with gold, making the art even more beautiful and valuable." I continued stirring the pot in front of me, smiling. I hadn't stopped smiling all day.

"Aww, that is the sweetest damn thing I have ever heard!" Layla clapped her hands together. "I wish someone would tell me I was something like that. I think the best I've gotten is someone told me once that I was like a balloon. Flexible and full of air. I liked it then, but come to think about it, maybe he was trying to tell me I was an airhead," she huffed out. "Bastard."

"Ha! Well, he was a dumbass then, Layla. But I do like the kintsugi line. I'll give Jay points for that. He is only saying what we all already know though, Rox. You know it too. Don't pretend you don't know you're a badass," Betty said.

Nikki had a far-off look in her eyes. "I like Jay so far. I think he's a keeper. But what's his flaw? He can't be perfect. None of them are even close. What's he hiding?"

"Well, we haven't gotten that deep yet. He hasn't anyway. I've told him some things about my past, but he clams up and is very vague about his life. Also, he is much more vanilla and reserved than what I would usually go for," I said.

"Hmm. Well, I think maybe you need more vanilla and reserved after your last relationship. I think he came into your life for a reason. Maybe to balance it out. Divine intervention!" she whispered the last two words.

We all groaned.

"Don't say it's not true. Things are all coming together for us, and it's because of the smudging and the crystals and the spells!" Nikki waved her hand in the air, motioning with an invisible magic wand.

"Don't you be doing that shit to me. I don't want involved in any spells! That's a one-way ticket to crazy town. I don't need any more demons. None of us do. You'd better keep it at crystals and your smoke sticks. No voodoo dolls, no séances, no spells, no crazy shit. We're all crazy enough!" Betty shook her head at Nikki.

"Didn't hear you complaining when I slipped that enchantment on Terrance at brunch," Nikki muttered under her breath.

"Please. I thought you were drunk and singing. He was enchanted because of my amazing personality and big, fat titties." Betty cupped her breasts, holding them up to her neck before tearing her palms away and letting them drop. Like a mic drop, but it was a boob drop. It wasn't her first time performing one.

"Sometimes, it really is like that though." Layla shrugged her shoulders.

We couldn't help but laugh.

"I'll figure out his flaw. I have an opportunity to see him again. Throw him in some situations. Get him to talk. We'll see." I winked at my girl gang and continued beaming while future dates with Jay played through my thoughts.

I arrived home late again. My date at Westy's was only a few days away, and as much as I had tried to catch up on sleep, I had been pulled in every direction lately. I glanced in my bathroom mirror, pushing the corners of my eyes up in hopes that they would stay there. They didn't. I felt this year had aged me threefold. I would be thirty soon, and already, the crow's-feet were starting to show up. They couldn't be smile crinkles. I hadn't smiled often enough.

I growled at my stubborn skin, insisting it stop aging so damn fast, and made a mental note to drink more water and get myself healthier.

Yeah, right.

I shuffled my feet across the floor toward my bed. My guest bedroom had become my sanctuary after Tommy. The master bedroom down below held too many bad memories, so I had transformed the guest room into my safe space. This room was where I'd written most of my poetry, and I had never let any men in here until Jay. I stopped in front of my window, lifting the blinds and peeking out at his window, wondering if he was fast asleep.

A light shone in his room, just as it had the last time I came home super late. That time, he had sung to me the sweetest of songs. He probably thought he had put me to sleep, but what he really did was rile me up. I totally rubbed one out after I hung up the phone with him. I had wanted to ask him over that night, but I also hadn't wanted to come off as a needy clinger.

But tonight, I could use some clinging. I sent a quick text to Jay.

> *Me: Can't sleep again?*
>
> *Jay: Your list has me anxious. It's keeping me up.*
>
> *Me: Really?*
>
> *Jay: No, not really. Maybe just a little. Do you know I've never been on a roller coaster?*
>
> *Me: Wow! You're … what, 30, 31? And never been on one?*

I tried to flip the conversation, so he'd start telling me more about himself. I grew tired of talking about myself all the time.

> *Jay: 32. My mom was a bit overbearing. She never trusted rides at the amusement parks. We never really went because of it. I have been to a circus, but amusement parks and carnivals and such, not really. I am not trusting of them either.*

Mommy issues. Bingo, I thought.

> *Me: Do you want me to change the treaty? We can do something else. I don't want you worrying yourself.*

> *Jay: No way! We made a deal. Plus, I already have your items to check off too. Would you like to hear them? Up for a call?*

> *Me: Yep.*

My phone buzzed in my hand, immediately sending butterflies fluttering about my insides. I braced myself for Jay's voice. That accent of his would be the death of me. He could tell me to go clean toilets, and I would do it with my panties off.

"Hey there, Kintsugi," he said. His words came out in a smooth melody, sultry and low.

I slid my panties off and threw them across the room.

"Hey." I smiled. "How was your day?"

"The usual. Busy as ever. But I've had you running through my mind the entire time. When things got crazy, I could feel your sunshine. You've set up camp in my brain. I keep replaying our rendezvous. The way you looked up at me with half-lidded eyes. That is etched into my soul."

Fuck, he has a way with words. He's going to nail his poem.

"I liked that too. A lot. So much that I'd like it more often." My voice shook as I tried to catch my breath. I closed my eyes and listened to his breathing.

"How about I do something for you tonight? It won't be part of the list, but it's still something I'd like to do. I want to try it out. For both of us."

"Another song?" I grinned, hoping he would sing me something dirty.

"I want you to touch yourself while I give you instructions on how to do it."

Even better, I thought.

My eyebrows rose into my hairline, wrinkling my forehead. I would age another year if he kept making me feel this way. I couldn't hide my expressions. He made me feel alive.

"Sounds like my kind of bedtime story. Whatcha got?" I acted innocent, as if I hadn't already had my hand between my legs as soon as he called me Kintsugi.

"First, I want you to slip your knickers off … slowly." His command rolled softly off his tongue.

"Okay," I agreed.

I did not want to embarrass myself by telling him it was already done and done. Besides, he'd said knickers.

Fuck. My toes curled.

"Good girl. Now, I want you to spread your legs apart and take your fingers and run them up and down the inside of your thighs. Back and forth. There, that's it. Gradually waking up your body."

My body was already awake and on edge, but I did as he'd said without question. My back arched, and my hips rolled. I needed him to break down my door and ravish me.

"Now, slowly start to circle your clit and then bring that hand back up to circle your nipple. Gently squeeze it for me, imagining I am taking it between my teeth and tongue."

Fuck.

"Bring those fingers back down and dip them inside of you. Tease yourself for me, fantasizing it's my cock. Are you wet for me? I want to hear how wet you are. Lower the phone and let me hear you play."

I was a fucking lake. Not a puddle. Not a pond. A lake. Maybe even an ocean here in a second.

I lowered the phone down, breathing heavy as I twirled my fingers between my legs, letting him listen to every slick sound.

"Fuck, that's good. You are so good. I want you to dip your fingers into yourself, getting them wet and bringing them up to your breasts. Trace a *J* there for me. That's it. I want you to mark my initial all over you."

My legs began to twitch as I traced his initial over my chest.

"Are you tracing them on your body? Around your navel and back down to your thighs," he asked.

"Mmhmm," I murmured.

"Start to circle your clit for me. Faster. Imagine it's my tongue exploring you. Fuck, you taste so good," he growled.

I heard his breath quicken and a slight slapping noise coming from his end of the phone.

"Are you—" I began to ask.

"Yes. I need you. I love the way your pussy clenches onto me. I'm thinking about that right now while I tease myself. You have me so close, so quickly."

"Damn, that's hot."

"You're hot. You're fire. My fire, Kintsugi. Keep circling your clit—faster now. I want to hear you come for me. Can you do that?"

My heart raced, as I knew that he was only a window away, tugging at that never-ending cock of his while imagining me. I wanted to climb that damn window and hop on him then and there. But I didn't have the time. I was damn near about to fall off my bed when the waves hit me. I felt the bubbles begin in my toes and start to travel up my legs as my thighs twitched outward across my bed.

"I'm there. I'm on edge. I'm ready," I growled.

"Fuck, I love that pussy of yours. I want to come together. I'm on edge too. I need to hear you come. Think of me pushing inside of you and filling you up. I need to fill you up. I ache for it. I want to drip down your thighs and trace my initials on you."

"Mmm," was the last sound I could make before my breath caught in my chest, and I let it all out in one loud cry. "Jay …"

"Oh, honey, my Kintsugi, I'm coming," he moaned loudly into the phone, his voice catching on each syllable.

The next few moments were a blur of moans, breaths, panting, and … *late-night television?*

A television in the background blared a laugh track, jolting me out of my trance.

"Sorry! Sorry! My foot flinched and kicked the remote, setting the television off." He laughed.

"That's okay. I like the laughs. It could have been worse. It could have been one of those *womp-womp* sound effects. Perfect timing, I'd say." I giggled.

"I like it when you laugh. If twinkling stars made a noise, it would sound exactly like your giggles."

I sighed into the phone and melted into my bed. "Thank you for that. It was fun. You're all the fun. And Westy's will be fun. No pressure, just fun. By the way, what is my list? You didn't tell me."

"Right. I got a little carried away. Mine is easy. I want to cook for you at Scarlett Herb on a date, I want to take you on one of my morning runs, and I want you to try Vegemite. Americans don't like that, but I think you will."

"I'm glad you told me this after what we just did. Otherwise, that would have been a total lady-boner killer. I can let you cook for me, no problem, but I don't exercise. I hope you know CPR if you expect me to run. Also, I heard Vegemite is of the devil."

I pinched the bridge of my nose and squinted my eyes. He would think I was weak sauce if I exercised next to him.

"No pressure. I'll go slow. I like it like that anyway."

"I know you do. When shall I sign up for this boot camp?"

"Tomorrow morning. It's supposed to be drizzling. Hearing the raindrops on the leaves is serenity in and of itself. But with the endorphins from our jog, I think you'll be in heaven."

"Tomorrow!" I shrieked.

"Better get to sleep there, sunshine. I'll be at your door at six. You can do it. You're tough as nails. But if you feel like you need more sleep, I don't want to pressure you. I know we are both up late. I just thought tomorrow would be—"

"I'm not as tough as nails. I'm as tough as a fucking railroad spike. You don't have to doubt me. I'll have my running shoes on at six sharp."

I hoped I had running shoes somewhere in the mountain of crap that was my closet.

"Perfect. I'll see you then. Good night, gorgeous." His voice alone made saying good-bye a lullaby.

"Good night, Jay. See you in the morning."

I laid the phone beside me and sighed, stretching my arms and legs out. A jog tomorrow morning sounded exhausting, but I wasn't one to back down. I had told myself I wanted to drink more water and get healthier. Maybe this was just another one of those divine intervention things that kept happening. Maybe Jay was in my life to not only pick me up, but to give me six-pack abs too.

I laced up the shoes I hadn't worn since college when my doorbell rang. I glanced down at my watch and read the time—two minutes before six o'clock. I groggily shuffled my feet across my hardwood floor toward the front door and opened it to a beaming face. Jay's glowing face. His face that I would like to see beaming up at me from between my legs.

I took him all in before I could say anything. I bit my lip, noticing the outline of his cock under his gray gym shorts and the sexy way that his white tee clung to his muscular chest. His nipples stiffened from either the spring chill or me. I hoped it was me. Mine stiffened too.

"Here you go. I'm afraid I don't know how you like it, so I just put a dash of sugar and cream in there." Jay handed me a cup of coffee. "It's Australian. From Melbourne, to be exact. We have the best coffee in the world. Not any of that hot bean water you guys sell down here."

"Oh, is that so? Well, I've survived on hot bean water so far." I brought the cup to my nose and breathed in the steam before taking a sip. "Wow, this is good! Not bitter at all. I could probably drink it black. Thanks. Come in. I am just going to put my hair up, and I'll be ready."

I motioned for Jay to follow me inside. My house wasn't immaculate, but I also didn't care. I was rarely here anyway. The only room I stayed in was the room upstairs. My five-star hotel room, he had called it. Everything else in here didn't get as much attention. I didn't like this house much and never wanted to get too attached to it or else I couldn't leave, and I did hope to leave one day. I just wasn't ready yet.

"How long have you lived here?" he asked.

"Oh, let's see … I moved here at twenty-four, and I'm twenty-nine now so … five years! Wow, it feels longer than that." I rolled the hair tie from my wrist and stuffed my hair into the lumpiest mess of a ponytail I could muster up this morning.

He walked over to the gallery wall that I had designed last year with the girls' help. We repaired the holes in the walls and taken down old pictures I didn't want to see anymore. The girls insisted that we turn the wall into a gallery of love. I'd hung some of my poetry, and they'd found silly pictures to hang, such as a unicorn flipping us off. In the center of the wall hung a picture of all of us together in front of the taco truck, holding a big DTF sign, hand-painted by Nikki's artist friend. The sign also hung on the gallery wall.

"I bet those five years have gone by fast with friends like these. It looks like you all have heaps of fun in whatever you're doing." He laughed, nodding toward the picture of us four in our T. rex costumes, lounging by Layla's pool.

We'd had a planned photo shoot that day, but instead, we'd fucked off, day-drinking. It was one of my best memories.

"DTF always has fun. It's not always been easy, but I'm grateful for them."

"You're fortunate. It's not easy finding one good friend, let alone three. I can tell by the way they came into the restaurant that day that they love you. One wrong move, and Betty told me she would skin me alive."

"No worries. I'll knock you out first." I finished my coffee and set the empty cup on the counter.

"If you can catch me. Ready to hit the trails?" He reached out, taking my hand and pulling me toward the front entry.

The second his skin touched mine, I felt my breath catch again.

"I'm ready for anything." I followed him out the door, locked it, and took a deep breath.

I hadn't worked out in a year or two—or ever. My running shoes weren't used for running. I'd bought them for walking across college campus years back when I took a few courses. I had never graduated, just like I had never worked out. I'd failed at both, and so far, I was okay with that. Business was good, my body was good, life was good.

"Let's go," he said, picking up his pace as we entered the woods.

The rain misted down around us, chilling the air and making my cheeks dewy.

I huffed my breath out from between my teeth as my feet hit the dirt.

"This is fun," I said while hopping over a branch that had fallen in the path.

"It is. We're about to start uphill. Let's see if we can get those endorphins flowing."

His breath became heavy as he pounded down on the dirt. I tried to match his rhythm by pushing my feet down into the earth harder, too, but I only made myself look like a jackass, stomping around. I much preferred this weird skipping thing I did.

I caught him side-eyeing me and smiling as I tried to figure out what the fuck I was doing. Whatever it was, I was having fun. All of my senses were being stimulated out here in the open. The scent of the pine trees, the feel of the wet air on my lips, the sound of the occasional bird chirping from the treetops, the sight of the sexy-as-fuck man working up a sweat next to me—all of it made my whole being feel alive. I wondered why I hadn't worked out before, and then we began our uphill climb.

It started with a side stitch. At least, that was what I thought it was called. It felt like a knife had jabbed into the side of my lung, lurching my breath up and out into a stifled grunt.

"You okay? Want to stop?" Jay smirked, still jogging at an even pace.

"Never," I replied through gritted teeth.

My eyes squinted as I tried to change my breathing from what sounded like a drowning hyena to something sexier. It didn't work. My breath only came out rattled and choking. He slowed down his pace and stopped.

"Come here, my little tough-as-a-rail-spike badass. You've got a cramp. I can tell."

"How. Do. You. Know?" I managed to huff out before locating the nearest log and plopping myself down on it, which hurt too. I cringed and rubbed my butt while simultaneously clutching my chest.

"Your breathing changed, and you look like you've been kicked in the vagina," he said. His eyebrows pulled together as a look of concern flooded his face.

"Shit. Yes. Although it feels more like I've been kicked in the lungs." I breathed in as deep and steady as I could.

"That's all right. We can take it slower. Slower is good. I think you'll be more comfortable with that anyway." He raised one eyebrow and sat next to me. He wasn't even out of breath.

"I liked it slow with you. Anyone else, and I would have had to pat their butt and tell them to *giddy up*. But you … you know how to touch me." I ran my hand down his exposed leg and back up his thigh. I saw his dick stir from under his gray shorts.

"You're so fucking gorgeous. Even when you're struggling not to die," he said before kissing me. His tongue slipped over mine as he locked on to my mouth.

I was already out of breath from my weird skip-hop-run, but now, he made me completely breathless. He put his arms around me, pulled me on his lap, and lifted my shirt.

"Do you want to do this? Out in the open?" I asked.

"Did you really think I only wanted to come out here to run?" he growled, lifting my sports bra.

I threw my head back and moaned as he took my nipple into his mouth and gently bit down. His other hand cupped my breast as I rocked back and forth on his lap. The soft mist of rain began to turn into a drizzle. The woods were thick enough to shield us from the worst of it, but I still became soaked—in more ways than one.

I circled my arms around his waist, holding myself tight around him. I could feel his heartbeat racing against mine.

"Jay, fuck me. I'm on birth control, and if you don't have the Australian fuck flu, let's do it. Here. Now. I need you," I moaned above the thunder that rumbled in the background.

"Oh shit," he growled, lifting me and carrying me to a nearby tree.

I nibbled his ear and kissed his neck as he walked toward the back of the tree so that we no longer faced the trail. He put me down for a quick moment while I hustled out of my tiny shorts, stuffing them in my bra. I hopped back into his arms and wrapped my legs around his waist as he quickly pulled his never-ending cock out of his shorts.

The tree bark rubbed hard against my spine as he stepped into me. His cock, yet again, kept going and going and going. If I hadn't known shit about women's anatomy, I could have sworn that tickle in the back of my throat was his dick head teasing me from the inside out.

"Fuck," I said, grabbing the back of his shoulders as he pushed into me in long, slow strokes.

I raised my hips with each thrust he gave me. The rain began to pour, finding its way through the leaves and drenching us. Still, Jay didn't stop.

I clutched at him harder, the more slippery we became.

"I got you. I'm not going to let you fall. Nothing's going to hurt you," he whispered, still giving me the long, slow strokes.

I locked my eyes on his, nodding and relaxing my body into his arms. His hands cradled my ass, shielding my exposed bits from the scratchy tree bark.

We stared at each other, our breathing soft and in sync. A smile played across his lips each time I let out a little moan. This man touched me in a way that I'd never been touched before, and I wanted to let him do it again and again.

The thunder rolled overhead, and rain pelted down on us, but we kept moving together. I was convinced the earth could give way under our feet, and we would still be locked in the moment, doing the dirty.

"I want you, all of you, inside of me. Give it to me. I want to feel you drip down my thighs," I pleaded. I needed to watch him hold his breath as he spilled out into me. I wouldn't be satisfied with my cardio until that happened.

"My Kintsugi, I'm all yours." He smiled, diving in deep.

His breath caught in his chest, and I knew he was about to fire-hose me with his explosive cum.

I dug my fingertips into his shoulder blades just as he gave me that last final push.

Squeak, came a sound from our feet.

"Squirrel!" I pointed toward the perverted animal watching us a few feet away.

"Huh?" Jay's eyes grew wide as I felt him shrivel and fall out of me right before my eyes.

We both looked down at that sad sight before he pulled his pants up, grabbed my hand, and began to run.

"Come on!" he screamed at me, his eyes wild, his other hand flying up in the air.

I ran my naked ass behind him, screaming too. I had no idea why I was screaming. I thought maybe there was a bear behind me, scoping out that squirrel. I didn't want to stick around to find out. I didn't even look back.

"Go! Go! Go!" he shouted beside me.

I could barely keep up his pace. We were under attack.

"Is it a bear? Jay! I'm scared. What was that? A wolf?" I said between breaths.

We made it to a clearing on the top of the hill.

"A squirrel! Didn't you see it?" His voice rose three octaves too high, as if he had been kicked in the balls, which I was on the verge of doing to him.

"What?" I asked, not sure if I had heard him right. Surely, I hadn't.

"That rabid rodent! The bloody wanker! Fuck! He could have mistaken my nuts for … nuts! No wonder he was watching my balls. He was about to bite me!" He glanced around the clearing, quickly turning back and forth. "I think we're good. He's gone. Phew."

"Are you fucking kidding me?" I narrowed my eyes, took my shorts from where I had stuffed them in my bra, and hastily put them on. "You're telling me that you are afraid of squirrels? You stopped before you blew your load because a squirrel saw you?"

"I blew my load while running for my life! My shorts are about to be as sticky as fuck. But, yes, fuck that. Squirrels are little devils. We don't have those in Australia. Disgusting creatures! They are cute until they bite you and give you a disease that will make you wish you were dead!"

"Disgusting creatures? As opposed to the million and one dangerous things y'all have in Australia that you have to fight against killing you each time you leave the house? I read about that tree there! You come close to it, and it shoots needles at you."

"Not exactly, but—"

"Fucking hell, Jay. A squirrel? I thought a damn bear was attacking us!"

"We don't have those either in Australia."

"Just man-eating trees, Seymour!"

"Um …" He ran his hands through his soaking wet hair, slicking it back just like the way he had worn it that first time I saw him coming from work. "Who is Seymour?"

"Never mind! Come here. If your only fault is your fear of rodents, I can hang with that." I stepped into him, rising onto my tiptoes to kiss his lips.

"If you think that's my only fault, you're wildly mistaken. I also kick ice under the fridge rather than pick it up. I don't always put the toilet seat down, and also, I sneak candy into movies."

"Now, who is pushing who away?" I laughed, laying my head against his chest.

The rain tapered off to a drizzle. I listened to his heartbeat slow down as we stayed there, locked in an embrace.

"I've also never been able to step out of my comfort zone. I'm afraid to take risks, and I like to play it safe. I don't like sharing feelings or being vulnerable, like most men I know. Still, no excuse. I think my fear of opening up is one of the reasons my ex cheated on me and broke my heart. I'd broken hers without meaning to. She wanted more from me than I could give. After my parents passed in their accident, it woke me up. I traveled the world, hoping to throw myself into fear and take risks, so it would somehow fix my relationships in the future. That I would be fearless and I could take on anything, much less feelings. I wouldn't be cautious, going forward. But I was cautious. On the entirety of my trip, I was still me and still cautious. Especially now. I'm terrified something bad will happen to someone that I love. Like an accident or something. Like what happened to my parents. I was close to them. I don't want to lose anyone else. I have a feeling deep down in the pit of my stomach that I merely exist these days when what I really want … and need … is to live."

My heart raced faster than it had when we ran from Monster Squirrel. If I had known this was all it would take to get Jay to talk, I would have brought him into the forest sooner.

"You're still not scaring me away," I said, shaking my head.

"What if I said that I feel like I'm living when I'm with you? That you are outside of my comfort zone and you make me feel alive and excited and like I want to share myself with you? I want to share it all with you. I want to be with you. I feel like I've known you my whole life. You want to talk about divine intervention? After traveling the world, I know there's something bigger out there, helping us along. I believe in it all. I believe we met for a reason. I want this to keep going and hopefully turn into something more. Does that scare you away?" He peeled himself off of me and held me at arm's length, searching my eyes.

My chest tightened, and I wanted to run back down that hill, all the way home, into my five-star hotel bedroom so I could hide under the covers. No man had ever said anything like that to me before. I wanted to cry, scream, melt, and marry him, all in that instant. I wanted him to know that I felt the exact same way, but I was a hypocrite who also had trouble opening up, and I was terrified of losing him in one way or another too.

"Still doesn't scare me," I lied.

SEVEN

Jay

"**Y**ou told her about your irrational fear of squirrels?" Aiden raised his eyebrows and motioned for Terrance to refill our glasses.

It had been another hectic day and late night at Scarlett Herb.

"I hadn't planned on telling her. It just so happened that there was a squirrel there, staring at us getting frisky, and I freaked out!" I picked up my drink and circled my wrist, listening to the giant ice cube clink against the glass.

I'd recounted my time with Rox to Aiden, leaving out the fact that I had freaked out so bad that I came instantly in my pants, just like the time Rox had peeked into my window.

"So, you like her—a lot. I can tell. I haven't seen you this way before. But there's something you're itching to ask me too. I know it. Spill it." Aiden clinked his glass to mine and waited.

"I am going to bring her here to dine, and I want to make her night magical. I get the feeling she hasn't been spoiled in a very long time."

Ever, I thought.

"Easy-peasy. Is she bringing Layla?" Aiden asked.

"Or Betty?" Terrance chimed in.

"No, nope. None of that. It's only Rox. It's a night for her. You guys can make your own dates with them. I'm just asking for your help in making this night perfect. Next Friday. This weekend, we are heading to Westy's. So, it will need to be next."

"Westy's?" Aiden asked. "Isn't that the sketchy amusement park way over there past the state line? I thought you didn't like to ride rides. Did you try them on your travels or something?"

"Aye, that's it. It's a bit of a drive, so I'll probably get us a room or something there. I'll ask her. The amusement park was all her idea though. You know I can't stomach that stuff. But I will for her." I tipped back my drink and finished it.

"Okay. Well, good luck. We will get to work on next Friday. Any menu requests?"

"Carbs. Also, Vegemite." I crossed my arms and leaned back in my chair. These bar chairs had cost more than six months' rent from my first apartment.

"That's not going to get you laid," Aiden muttered.

"I want more than that anyway." I smiled, thinking about Rox's tattooed raven spreading its wings and flying off.

"Whatever you say." Aiden shook his head.

"I say, another whiskey, please. On the rocks." I held my drink up to Terrance for a refill.

"On the rocks." He grinned. "You got it, boss."

After we had decided that we would stay a night in a hotel nearby Westy's, I had packed my suitcase and set it by the front door, ready to take anything that Rox could throw at me. I hoped she would throw herself at me.

The last two nights, I had waited up to hear that familiar car door slam so that I knew she was home safe. She'd become more distant since I bit the bullet and told her how I thought we had met for a reason. Divine intervention sounded like a bunch of hoopla to me, too, but it was real.

Countless times, I had seen or experienced things that I couldn't explain. Traveling the world had given me a new perspective on that at least. I still had to trust myself too. I couldn't leave it all in the hands of the stars.

I stared into the dark, thinking of how I would get through tomorrow's thrilling adventure. I had packed ginger chews in case I had motion sickness, and I also packed Advil in case a stress headache hit me. Two pairs of underwear and some foot sprinkling for fresh soles in my shoes later, and I became a walking geriatric ward.

I flipped my pillow to the other side, cooling my face against the silken pillowcase. If Rox were here, I would probably sleep like the dead. Living next door to her was a blessing and a curse. I loved being close to her, but I hated her late nights at the shelter or wherever she was. I just wanted and needed her safe. Anxiety, worry, and bad dreams had kept me up at night ever since my parents' accident, and now, with Rox becoming such a source of light in my life, I didn't need her snuffed out too. I worried about her at the shelter. I didn't know much about her ex, Tommy, but I knew enough to feel that he wasn't someone I would ever want nearby her again.

I closed my eyes as I heard her car pull into her drive. The slammed door rang out throughout the night. I breathed a sigh of relief, and within moments, I fell asleep.

The next morning, I brought Rox the coffee she loved. She was already loading her car as I walked over and began to help.

"What's this? Your medicine bag? Would you like a walker too?" Rox asked, eyeballing my literal medicine bag.

"It's in case we get sick on the rides or something. There's a first aid kit in there too. I come prepared." I shrugged, suddenly feeling eighty-two.

"We're going to ride roller coasters, not fight an epidemic overseas. Do y'all have that over there? Crazy diseases to match your crazy wildlife?" She set my bag in the backseat of her tiny car and pulled me in for a kiss.

"Heaps of them! Like the Australian fuck flu," I whispered into her lips.

"Mmm … so glad you don't have that, and we can get frisky without getting risky! Let's go!" She slapped my ass and hopped into her car.

I walked around to the passenger side and slid in beside her.

I had looked up Westy's on the map the day before to check the drive time. Three hours. Three hours would be a perfect opportunity to show Rox my love for Australian rap music. Maybe she would love it too. I had meticulously planned out a playlist and hoped she was game to give it a try. I would sell it as part of the treaty.

"I thought you might like to try something else new. No squirrels or cardio involved this time." I strapped in and braced myself as she veered out of her driveway and hit the road.

"What's up? I'm down for anything. Today is going to be off the chain!" She grabbed the steering wheel and pulsated her body.

"Off the chain. Good. We are on the same page. I have some Australian rap music if you'd like to hear it. It's some of my favorite tunes. Can I connect to your Bluetooth in here?"

"You don't even have to ask. Fire it up. What do y'all rap about anyway? Koalas' chlamydia rates and those damn kangaroos?" She eased onto the interstate and leaned back, settling into her seat.

"No! Did you read about that? Those damn koalas are trouble. Kangaroos too. We rap about a lot of things. The struggle is as real there just as it is here." I fumbled around in my phone settings before finding the right connection and pushing play.

The music blasted through the car stereo. I tapped my fingers across my knee in rhythm with my favorite rap artists, bobbing my head and slanging drugs in my mind. I let three songs play before I lowered the volume and shot her a quizzical look.

"Pretty badass, isn't it?" I fist-pumped the air. I had no idea what that was, but I had seen Americans do it once years ago.

"Yeah. Yep. Badass." She nodded. Her lips pressed into a thin line as she held back whatever she felt.

"For real? You didn't like it! I can tell! You're choking back car sickness or disgust for my taste in music. Either way, I brought meds for that." I shook my head and put my phone down in my lap.

"I think I've found something we don't agree on. It wasn't bad! Maybe it will grow on me in time. I like rap, but I prefer rock. Here, listen. This is what I like. Let's kick this day off and get wild." She tapped the screen in front of her and pulled up a playlist titled Rock Out with Your Vag Out, scrolling through it until she landed on "I Love Rock 'n' Roll" by Joan Jett & the Blackhearts. She turned the volume up high enough to rattle the windows.

I nodded my head in agreement, ready to get wild with her. I could listen to this type of music. I had to gear myself up for roller coasters, tattoos, and sharing my feelings in poetry anyway. The edgy music worked to ease my way into this wild ride I'd somehow gotten myself into.

I watched her, mesmerized, as she belted out every lyric to the top of her lungs. Her lips parted wide in song, like a songbird—my raven. We raced toward Westy's in a melody of excitement and badassery. She took a breather in between songs and glanced over at me, catching me in my trance. When I caught her eye, she put her fist in the air, pinkie and index finger raised and stuck her tongue out over her knuckles. My cock thickened in my pants at the sight of her tongue. I knew she could probably do amazing things with it.

I stuck my fist in the air, parting my lips and returning the gesture.

Rock on.

We arrived at Westy's shortly after they opened. With Rox's speedy driving skills and only a quick stop through a drive-through for breakfast, we made quicker time than I'd thought we would. Much quicker. Too quick. The sight of a great roller coaster toward the back of the park turned my legs into Jell-O.

"You're as pale as a ghost." Rox laughed, handing me my ticket. "Here ya go! My treat. A treat for the treaty. Also, you look like you're about to faint. Do you need to sit down?"

I grabbed the ticket with my sweaty palm and shook my head. "Let's do this."

"Are you sure? I don't want to make you do anything you are scared to do."

"Who? Me? Scared?" I blew out a breath. "Never."

"Just of squirrels. Got it." She put her hand in mine and quickly pulled it back. "You are scared! Your hand feels like the inside of a clam! We can go slow. Let's do something easy first. Like the swing or the bumper car, or we can play a game! How about the Ferris wheel? That's an easy one. Let's go!"

"Sorry," I said, wiping my hands on my pants and following behind her.

Her arse bounced as she skipped along ahead of me. I focused on the bottom of her tiny jean shorts instead of the monstrous contraptions whizzing around me. If her shorts were much shorter, I could see my favorite spot on her—the place where her thighs met the curve of her arse. My dick twitched to the left, following right behind her as if it connected to some type of Rox radar.

"Where is my sexy jogger when I need him? What are you doing back there, Grandpa?" She stopped to wait on me before hooking her arm in mine and dragging me toward a Ferris wheel that looked like it was moments from spinning off its old axles and rolling straight through town.

"We're riding in that? That doesn't look safe! Look at all the rust! And that creaking noise! Is this the same amusement park I read about where those people got stuck upside down in that coaster?"

"No! Westy's isn't like that. It's old, but that is part of its American charm. This place has been around longer than me, but the owners keep it up-to-date. I think there is a new owner now—Westy's son, Weston. Maybe the younger generation will spruce it up a bit. It's safe though! Come on."

"Westy's and Weston," I repeated, shaking my head. "I am going to trust you on this. But if I get up there and we start to hamster-wheel off and end up in the river, I do get to say that I told you so."

The ride attendant, who looked as if he were twelve years old, nodded politely and ushered us into a large capsule. I put one foot in front of the other and stepped into the swaying bucket of death. My hands gripped the center pole as I squeezed my eyes shut. I let out a groan as we began to make our ascent. My eyes were still squinted shut when I felt Rox's hand on my dick.

"Quick. Whip out that cock and let me calm you. I've always wanted to do this!" She began unzipping my pants.

"I don't know what you're doing, but don't stop." I kept my eyes closed.

My fingers curled around the pole as I peeked from between my lashes before quickly squinting my eyes shut again. The bucket of death swayed in the air as Rox positioned herself in front of me … on her knees.

Fuck.

"Already hard. That's my man!" she cheered as she shoved my cock in her mouth.

The Ferris wheel stopped right as we made it to the top.

"What's happening?" I asked, keeping my eyes closed.

"I'm sucking your dick," she spit out before returning to work on my shaft.

"No, we're stopped. Fuck. That feels good. Why are we stopped?" The panic began to rise in my chest.

"Shh. It's normal. Relax. We're about to start again, and you're going to spend the entirety of our day with blue balls." She gripped her hand around the base of my cock, working me up and down and bobbing her head in matching rhythm—quicker and quicker.

I hung on to the pole, eyes still shut, when a gust of wind sent the bucket swaying forward. My heart raced as we began to move again. The bucket swayed back and forth, and I was too chicken to open my eyes and see what was going on. I only knew that my dick was out, and I was vulnerable as fuck and about to die.

Another gust of wind blew through the cart, sending me into a panic-induced explosion.

"Ahh!" I yelped as I immediately spilled out into her mouth.

My dick pulsed hard, matching the pulse of what felt like a minor heart attack.

"Fuck! Sorry. I usually give a warning. I just … I got scared and creamed my pants again." I opened my eyes and apologized as she swallowed hard and tucked my cock away, giving it a little pat.

"Not inside your pants. Inside my mouth. And you taste like pineapple. That's a bit weird, but I like it. You're a tropical drink. I hope that settles you a bit because we're just getting started with the fun." She scooted into me and kissed my cheek. Her lips were still wet.

I didn't have the heart to tell her I had been chugging pineapple juice since we fucked at her place. I hadn't had a blow job in years, and if I even remotely had the chance of getting one, I wanted to be prepared. A quick search on the internet had told me just how easy it was to sweeten my load. My pantry could have been mistaken for a pineapple farm. I had eaten the fruit, drunk the juice, and put that shit on everything.

Pineapple on my pizza?

Check.

Pineapple salsa?

Check.

Pineapple cocktails?

Check.

Chugging pineapple juice every waking moment I had?

Double check.

"That was incredible. You are amazing. A *Rox* star!" I put my arm over her shoulders and kissed the top of her head.

"Rox star. I like that. I prefer Kintsugi though. That hits me in the feels."

"And you like being hit in the feels?" I tilted my head, catching her eye, but she looked away.

"By you." She shrugged.

"I hope you enjoyed the ride!" The attendant smiled as he opened the gate and let us out of the death bucket that I had a new respect for.

Maybe later, I would even try to fuck her in it.

We walked through the park hand in hand, stopping at the bumper cars, a train that circled the entire park, and a funhouse where we snuck in a quick make-out session. Her tongue twirled around mine as I pushed her up against a mirror that made us both look stretched out. I wanted to turn her around and fuck her in that mirror as we watched our silly reflections staring back at us.

"Someone's coming," she whispered into my mouth.

We peeled ourselves off one another and continued through the park. I stopped to play a few games and do the chivalrous thing by winning her a stuffed animal, but she insisted that she was not the cuddly stuffed-animal type and instead told me I could buy her a corn dog.

"A what? You want a dog?" I asked.

"A corn dog! Don't you know what a corn dog is? I know it's not something you'd serve at Scarlett Herb, but it's like the all-American staple. Besides apple pie. It's that thing!" She pointed toward a sign hanging off of a truck.

"Oh! Yes, we have those. That's what we call a dippy dog, and they are delicious! I eat junk too, you know! Not everything I eat has to be sous vide or braised in something I can't even pronounce." I shook my head and put in an order.

My stomach had been growly, but I didn't want to eat before riding the coaster of doom. I also didn't want to see Rox hangry. My pulse quickened as I looked into the distance at the rickety railing on the track.

"You're stalling on that coaster, aren't you?" She hooked her arm around mine and smirked as we waited for our food. "It's not that bad. Plus, you'll get the same endorphin buzz you get when you do your jogging. It's like a runner's high, but you don't have to, you know … do anything, except sit on your ass and hang on for dear life."

"Sounds … pleasant." I flinched. "Fine. I'll get it over with. But so that you know, I've never done anything like that in my life. Thrill rides or anything other than slow and steady is just not me. I might pass out or … jizz in my pants again."

"Yeah, yeah. I know. You're Mr. Safety. I promise it's safe."

We took our grease on a stick and sat down at a shaded picnic table. Watching her lips circle that dippy dog brought me back to the Ferris wheel when I had been too chicken to watch. Now, I was kicking myself. Rox's lips on my throbbing cock was a memory I would need to see over and over again—on replay. That would be good wanking material.

I took a bite of my corn dog, wondering if I looked as sexy as she did when I ate it. I hoped not. I bit into it hard and yanked it from my mouth as if I were tearing a steak in two, finishing it in only a few quick bites. Her eyebrows furrowed as we sat in silence, watching each other. She stuck her tongue out and licked the entire corn dog's length and winked at me. My balls vibrated as I watched her tongue expertly slide up and over and back down that meat stick.

"You should have opened your eyes," she said, ferociously biting into the corn dog and breaking my gaze.

"I was thinking the same thing. I wish I had."

"Maybe you'll get another chance. We have all night at Westy's Inn."

"Westy's Inn? That is the hotel? Owned by the same people?" I tapped the end of my corn dog's stick on the table.

"Yep. They own a diner too. Best fluffernutter around!"

"You Americans and your crazy food terms. I don't know what a fluffernutter is, but I hope I can do it tonight!"

She nodded, swallowing the last of her food. "Shenanigans all day and all night. I'll buy you a fluffernutter and then give you my version of a fluffernutter. You'll have to hang on to something though. I'm wilder than any of these rides."

"Don't I know it!"

Her smile grew from ear to ear as she leaned over the table to kiss me. "Let's go to the petting zoo before we ride the coaster. Not sure I want to ride The Comet after I just ate that." She shivered, clenching her teeth. "The Vomit Comet. That's what they call it. But we'll be fine. It's safe. Plus, you got your meds if motion sickness is an issue."

"That sounds like a terrible time, but I'm trusting you. The endorphin high is tempting. Especially since I missed my morning run."

"No worries. Cardio coming later." She squeezed my arse and bit her lip.

I couldn't fucking wait.

The petting zoo smelled like a petting zoo. The animals looked well enough, but the scent that lingered in the air singed my nose hairs. We entered into a tiny barn, and I almost fell over, dizzy with disgust. Rox and I side-eyed each other because the smell in the barn was like that of raw sewage, eggs, and cow patties, all left out in an Australian heat for a fortnight.

"It's Daisy here. She's had a bit of a problem lately," the handler said, smacking the rump of a cow. "We're tweaking her diet, but you'll have to excuse the cloud of funk surrounding her. Poor thing is sick."

Rox put her hand over her mouth. Her face became a putrid shade of green.

"What's a matter? Fart barn scaring you away?" I asked, reaching out to stroke Daisy's back.

Rox's eyes crossed as she backed away and turned to leave, stifling both laughter and nausea with her palm. She breathed in deeply as soon as we stepped into the fresh air.

"I'm extremely sensitive to smells! That animal was dying! I couldn't handle it there. Especially after I just ate! I guess you got something on me now. Yes, I'm unable to handle certain smells. My gag reflex triggers easily." She put her nose in the air and took another deep breath.

"I'd say your gag reflex works just fine. But let's get away from this place. How about we play some games?" I asked.

"How about you not stall any longer and we catapult ourselves through the sky on The Comet? Dum, dum, dum!" She lowered her voice, opened her arms wide, and tried her best to sound scary. She only sounded like a mouse.

It was cute but no way I would tell her that. I pretended to shake in fear.

"I'm ready." I grabbed her hand and kissed the back of her knuckles. "Let's fly through the air, little raven."

As we neared the nonexistent line for The Comet, my anxiety began to get the best of me.

What if I get sick up there?
What if I get stuck up there?
What if I plummet to the ground?
What if it collapses?

I gripped Rox's hand with my sweaty palm and faintly followed her to the first row of seats.

"I got us the best seats! You can see everything from up at the top. You can see what's coming up ahead too. Like those double loops or that swirly-whirly part of the track."

I pushed the bulky brace into place as tight as I could, making me barely able to breathe under pressure. I would much rather suffocate under this contraption than be propelled forward into the sky and across Westy's. I closed my eyes and steadied my breathing, mentally preparing myself for what would come next.

"Hey, Jay? Are you okay? You're all of a sudden quiet. We don't have to—" She reached down and squeezed my knee as soon as the coaster lurched forward.

"I'll be okay," I squeaked out as we climbed up the creakiest track I'd ever heard.

"Change to the treaty! One quick change!" she spit out. "Gotta keep your eyes open!"

I couldn't see her from around the shoulder braces, but I was pretty sure she was trying to make sure I had them open.

"That's an unfair rule change! You can't do it at the last minute!" I cried, still squeezing my eyes shut.

The coaster paused at the top of the first drop.

"Do it! I promise you'll love it! Just this once! Open them! Quick! Keep 'em open!" she shouted.

I flung my eyelids open like the good sport I was and immediately came in my pants—or at least, I hoped that was cum. My dick convulsed as I screamed like a bitch while the coaster dived straight down. I kept my eyes open, following the tracks and crying out like a five-year-old girl at a boy band concert. Whatever weird noises I made had Rox laughing harder than I'd ever heard anyone laugh before in my life. If anything, I was glad I could entertain her.

We hit the whirly thing she'd warned me about, and I let out another girlish scream. She began snort-laughing next to me. We whizzed through the loops and spun through the twirls while my stomach plummeted into my balls and my heart was in my throat. I didn't even bother to close my mouth the entire time because I couldn't stop screaming, no matter how hard I fought with my voice to shut the fuck up.

A bright flash from a mounted camera zapped my eyes as we hurled toward the end. As the gates became closer, my tension became looser. The roller coaster slowed to a stop, and my entire body came alive. I felt like I could hold all of the air in the world in my lungs, swim across the sea to back home, and tackle whatever anyone threw my way.

The braces bounced up, and we clambered out of our seats and made our exit. My legs and voice still shook, but my soul wanted to ride again. I looked over at Rox, who had stopped laughing and hobbled down the path.

"That was thrilling! Amazing! I understand it all now! I'd love to go again!" I jumped into the air, quickly composing myself as I remembered the moist stickiness in my pants.

"I peed a little," she whispered, slumping her shoulders forward.

"Come again?" I wasn't sure I'd heard her right.

"I peed my pants. Fuck! It's just a sprinkle of a tinkle, but fucking hell, you had me laughing so hard. Now, we have to go! I've got to change. Let's go to a hotel."

"Oh. Right! That's all right. I came in my pants, so we are even. I do want to run and get our picture right quick if you don't mind. And pick up some fairy floss to take back." I put my arm around her shoulders. The endorphin high pulsing through my body made me feel as if Rox and I could take on the world, messy pants and all.

"Yes! I want the picture too. What's fairy floss?" she asked.

"Cotton candy! Want to load up on a bunch of junk and stay in the hotel for the rest of the night, eating crap and fucking around? I mean, I already came three times today, but I'm down for more."

"Best plan ever! Just let me shower." She cringed, adjusting her shorts. "And, Jay?"

"Yes, dear?"

Dear? Why did I say that?

That word had come out so natural and felt so right. She didn't even flinch.

"Did you like doing that? Soaring through the sky like a bird? Did it make you feel good and tingly? Besides the tingles from when you jizzed your pants? Did I convert you to liking to go wild and fast?" She stopped walking and turned to meet my eyes.

"I think I like flying wild, fast, and free with my raven. I had fun, and I'm excited to see what else your clever brain can come up with for me—or us." I tilted her chin up to mine and pressed my lips to hers.

EIGHT

Rox

The first thing I did Monday morning when Betty had offered to pick me up in the taco truck was show her the picture of Jay and me on the roller coaster and tell her I'd pissed my pants.

"You pissed your pants? Oh no. Hold up. The Rox I know isn't scared of a damn roller coaster. What made you piss your pants? Did he scare you or something? I told him I'd make his Crocodile Dundee ass into an alligator bag!" Betty clutched the steering wheel and shook her head. Her long hair flowed behind her as she sped down the street.

The weather had been warm enough for us to keep our windows open, and all of us preferred the fresh air to the scent of tacos all day long. It became old after a while.

"No! I pissed my pants because I was laughing at him. He screamed like a bitch! It was hilarious. Also a little sexy. I swear, with that accent, he could do anything, and I'd throw my panties at him."

"Not your pee panties, I hope! Unless that's a kink of his. How else did the date go? Did you have a good night? Did he treat you right?"

"Hard pass on the pee fetish. It was amazing. We stayed at Westy's Inn. It was pretty sketchy, but that didn't stop us from having fun all night. It was—*he* was great." I leaned into the open window and let the air hit my face, remembering the rush of wind on my cheeks as we sped through the sky on The Comet.

"What's next for y'all? It seems like you're both headed down this road pretty fast."

"I don't know. He's going to cook for me at Scarlett Herb on Friday night, and I'm sure we will see each other a lot over this week since you know … he lives right freaking next door! He waits up for me. Did I tell you that? He wants to know I'm safe, so he waits until he hears me pull in the drive. I can see his light on upstairs. It turns off when I shut my car door. I've never had anyone care like that."

"I know you haven't. Are you sure he is caring, or is he controlling? He might be waiting up to see if you come home at night. As in if you're out with another man. Or maybe he wants to see if you are bringing home another man. Maybe this is one of those gaslighting things."

"No. At least, I'm pretty sure that isn't the case." I closed my eyes, concentrating on the last few times he had stayed up and our phone conversations after.

Did he ever mention me being out with another man? Did he fish for information? He sounded genuinely concerned, didn't he?

My stomach fluttered as a traumatic memory with my ex, Tommy, surfaced. I shook my head and pushed it back, focusing on Jay.

"His parents were in a terrible car accident. I think that is where the worry comes from when he stays up, wondering. He is Mr. Safety all the way. He is almost too safe. Not my style at all. But I think he had a good time, and I'm rubbing off on him. He already asked when we were going back to Westy's. He said we should bring his brother and DTF."

"Sounds like a fun time to me. I'm glad Jay's safe, but you'd better be sure that is what it is. Layla told me about his parents. She and Aiden have been spending time together, working on the Shizzle Sauce. Aiden opened up to her."

"Really? Jay hasn't talked much about his personal life. He's said a few things here and there, but he struggles with being vulnerable. Guess that flaw doesn't run in his family then."

Betty side-eyed me and pursed her lips together in a thin line. "We're picking her up today, too, after Nikki. You can ask her about it. But, Rox?"

"Yeah?"

"If someone sounds too good to be true—" she started.

"They usually are," I sighed.

The following week had been our busiest yet. The Pink Taco Truck sold out every single night before seven thirty. Layla went back to Scarlett Herb, making Shizzle Sauce three times already. She swore up and down that she was making Shizzle Sauce and not banging Aiden, who she claimed was just a friend.

She gave me a heads-up on Friday's dinner, telling me that Aiden and the crew had been preparing it all week. Jay wanted to go all out for me and show me just as good of a time as I had shown him. I wasn't so sure about Scarlett Herb. I owned a freaking taco truck, for crying out loud. My dinners were never shit I couldn't pronounce that had been flown in from somewhere I also couldn't pronounce. But I trusted Jay to make it right.

We texted off and on throughout the week, but both of us were too busy to meet up. I worked late every single night and then headed to the shelter, and he was gone every single morning when I woke up. I didn't even have much time to write poetry these days, which reminded me of the treaty we had agreed upon. He still owed me a tattoo *and* a poem. I texted him during our after lunch lull.

> Me: *Any thoughts on what your tattoo will be? Have you started your poem?*
>
> Jay: *Yes! The tattoo anyway. The poem ... not so much. I will show you what I'm thinking about tomorrow night. Are you ready for a dinner date with me? I realize we haven't done the regular dates yet, and I'm keen to take you out properly even if it's here at my restaurant.*
>
> Me: *I'm keen to be taken out properly. Wine me, dine me, 69 me.*
>
> Jay: *You know I will.*
>
> Me: *I know you will.*

"Why are you smiling over there?" Nikki came around the back of the truck and stretched her long legs. She'd been dancing even more at The Steamy Clam.

"I was texting Jay. What's up with you? Any new favorite customers at the club?" I sat down on a curb and patted the pavement next to me. "Sit. Catch me up on everything."

"Betty is still Betty, busting every man's balls from here to there. Layla has been getting closer and closer to Aiden, but they haven't dated yet, she said—or fucked. Not sure if I believe that. Earl is supposed to come by the next poetry night. He wanted to talk to us about some ideas for a seasonal menu change. Social media is going well. Our followers do most of the work with retweets. And me … I'm still working the pole and being a badass and praying to the Goddess of Dick that I can get some soon."

"No prospects at all?" I raised my brows.

Nikki was a player. She always had a man in her back pocket.

"Oh, there've been prospects. But no one has yet taken my breath away, and I'm not settling until I find someone who does. The others are only my toys." She reached up, clutching her crystal necklace in her palm.

"I know what you mean about taking your breath away. I've never felt that way before, but Jay … he does it to me. And he is so reserved and classy. Not sure why I am so drawn to him. He's not even close to my type!"

"What do you mean, drawn to him?" She tilted her head sideways, studying my face.

"Like, I want to eat, sleep, and breathe him. I'm so comfortable with him, like I've known him my entire life. He's been gentle and kind to me, and he's concerned about my well-being. Usually, most men want to fuck and then head out. They always, always head out too. All of them. Mentally or physically."

"Like Tommy," she whispered.

"Like Tommy. His mind became a big black hole. I'm still not sure what happened, but I feel like he sucked the light out of me. And Jay? He's funneling that light back in."

"The light's been there, Rox. You are the light. No one can give it to you because you are already it. Jay's just opening your eyes. He is here for a reason, and I believe that reason is to get you to see yourself as the world sees you. Not as what Tommy told you that you were. I know it's hard to heal from that. But look at you! You're smiling. I don't know where this all is going for you and Jay, but wherever it goes, it will be worth it. You're healing yourself. Jay is just the catalyst. Right place and the right time." She slipped something smooth and hard into my palm. "Rose quartz. For love. I see it. You're falling in love."

"Falling in love, huh? You think a rock will make me and Jay fall in love?"

"I didn't mean falling in love with Jay. I meant falling in love with yourself." Nikki rose to her feet and leaned down to kiss my forehead.

"That was pretty fucking deep." I poked the crystal around in my hand.

"Sometimes, I can get deep. I've seen a lot of shit."

"No doubt about that. Thanks, Nikki. I guess we'd better prep for dinner."

"What are you two doing back there?" Layla poked her head out from the front of the truck.

"Having a *come to Jesus* meeting!" I answered.

"Is that a church thing? I didn't know y'all went to church!" Layla's mouth dropped open.

"Their hair would catch on fire the moment they walked in there if they did. Come on. Let's start prep!" Betty said, coming around the corner to see what we were up to. Her eyes traveled to the crystal clutched in my hand. "That'd better be to ward off assholes. It's looking a little too pink and rosy to me."

"No worries. My clever brain is warding off assholes," I snapped back in my best Australian accent. I sounded as if I'd been day-drinking and had a scratchy throat.

"Clever? Oh Lawd! Haven't heard that word come out of your mouth before. Next thing I know, you'll be serving champagne and coq au vin out of this taco truck. Or better yet, you'll want to open some fancy-schmancy place with white tablecloths and chandeliers." Betty rolled her eyes.

"Oh my gosh! Yes! That sounds fantastic!" Layla squealed next to her, hopping up and down.

"No. Just no." Betty shook her head at both of us and returned to work.

"You know she worries so much about you. She never wants to see you stuck with someone like Tommy again," Nikki whispered.

"I know. I don't ever want to see me with an asshole again either. Jay isn't like that though. He wouldn't hurt a fly. He's so … kind," I whispered back to her.

"Good. Betty will come around. Maybe he should spend a date night with DTF, and she can see what you see." Nikki opened the back door to the truck, letting me inside.

"That sounds terrifying, but I'll see what I can do," I told her before stepping inside.

I turned my music up and stepped into the shower. I wanted to make sure that, tonight, I would come across as classy as fuck—even with my inked sleeves. Layla had helped me pick out my silky bronze dress, Nikki had let me borrow her sexy black pumps, and Betty had passed me a small keychain bottle of mace. Even though my taco truck worked with Scarlett Herb, I'd yet to set foot in there. With the way Layla had described his place, it sounded like I would be heading to a royal palace. But Nikki and Betty had only shrugged and said Jay's restaurant was nice.

I had never eaten at a fancy restaurant before. My taste buds preferred hard liquor, greasy burgers, and buckets of chili cheese dip. I had also never picked up a wine menu or ordered anything I couldn't pronounce. And according to Jay, Scarlett Herb offered things on their list that I would need to Google before ordering. I wouldn't want to order something that sounded tasty and ended up being a fish paste, which he had told me was divine and on their menu. No, thanks.

I lathered up my legs, shaving off everything I had while rocking out to classic rock. My blood pumped through my veins in a mixture of excitement and nervousness. I wasn't a nervous type of woman, but Jay had me up in my feels like a giggly schoolgirl. One whisper in my ear with that hot-as-fuck accent of his, and I wanted to put my hand to my heart and faint. He was that good.

When I had texted him the other night about the new case at the shelter, he'd asked if I wanted to talk about it. When I had said yes, he called me immediately. He listened to my rough night and then sang me a lullaby to sleep. Yep, he sang to me again. His voice alone could calm me and set me on fire, all in one. It had become a ritual over the last week—his light shutting off when I pulled in the driveway or us talking on the phone before bed. He had invited me over a few times, but it was so late that I'd made every excuse in the book not to give in. I also was beginning to feel nervous about how close we were becoming so quickly.

I still needed to feel Jay out. Betty had said his worrying over me could really be control, and that was not something I ever wanted to deal with again. He genuinely seemed concerned about my well-being, but just in case, I wanted to take this slow, and so far, I had been doing the opposite. I was falling into him hard and fast—at my usual pace.

I finished showering and toweled myself off in front of the mirror. My fingers traced around my tattoos. I hadn't exactly lied to Jay when he asked what they meant. Some of my ink did have sentimental meaning, but some of it didn't. He seemed too innocent, too gentle, and too kind to hear about the stories I'd marked myself with. Besides, I had told him about my raven, which, to date, was the most significant tattoo for me. I would never fall in love with an abusive asshole again. No way would I get stuck in that type of relationship. It was a vicious cycle I didn't like to look back on. Thankfully, that tattoo was in a place that I knew was there, but I didn't have to see it every day.

I rubbed the raven on the back of my neck, quieting the memories that were bubbling up. I pressed the volume up on my speaker and began fixing my hair and makeup. Jay had texted me earlier to let him know when I was ready and he would pick me up. I had offered to walk across the lawn, but he'd insisted on being a gentleman and doing this right.

Why is he so kind to me?
What does he want?

I glanced down at my buzzing phone and noticed the DTF group text blowing up. Layla needed help with Shizzle Sauce, Nikki was busy working amateur night at The Steamy Clam, and Betty was out, taking her nieces to a movie. I quickly texted back Layla to schedule some of our substitute employees for the weekend and triple the batch, so we didn't have to keep under Scarlett Herb's feet. I hated to continue using their kitchen all of the time.

My phone kept buzzing, but I ignored it, turned it on Do Not Disturb, and began to curl my hair into big, voluptuous waves. I had no idea what I was doing, and right now, I looked as if I'd stuck my finger in an electric socket.

Fuck!

I brushed it out and grabbed my straightener. I didn't have time to experiment. Our reservations were soon, and I didn't want to keep Jay waiting. I finished up my hair and makeup and slid into my dress. I hadn't worn a dress in a while, or at least not a dress like this—silky, long, and low slung over my barely existing breasts. It had cost more than anything else I owned in my closet, but Layla had insisted it fit me like a glove, and I would wear it again in the future for weddings and stuff. I had no idea what she meant by weddings and stuff. All of my friends were happily single, and the *stuff* she referred to was either funerals or babies. Neither of which any of us were prepared to handle.

I switched my music off and double-checked myself in the mirror. If a biker chick got dressed to go to a ballet at the theater, this was what she would look like. I nodded at myself, impressed. I could do classy—kind of.

Jay pulled up to Scarlett Herb's front entrance and handed the special weekend valet his keys. The attendant opened my door for me as Jay waited on the curb to take my arm and walk me inside his establishment. The corners of his mouth were turned up in a prideful grin.

"Have I told you how gorgeous you are?" He took my hand and pressed the back of my knuckles to his lips.

"Oh, only about twelve times since we left my house. But I like it. Keep going." I stood on my tiptoes to peck him on the cheek.

We walked up the stairs to the oversize iron double doors. I wasn't sure if I was walking into a restaurant or a fortress.

"After you, Kintsugi." Jay opened the door and stepped aside to let me pass.

I paused inside the foyer, allowing my eyes to adjust to the low lighting. Betty should have put a flashlight on my keychain instead of mace.

"Mr. Taylor! We have your table ready. Right this way." A young hostess twinkled her eyes and motioned for us to follow her.

We walked past a crowded bar area and open-aired dining room, straight to the back where a row of cubby-like rooms were tucked into the walls. They were a few steps up, perched on a ledge, overlooking the dining area. Heavy drapes hung on either side of the doorways, some shut and others opened as the guests took their regal seats high atop the room.

The hostess pulled back the drapes to our room and held out her hand as if to say, *Voilà!*

Wow.

The table had the most beautiful bouquet I'd ever seen. The flowers ranged in shades of reds and deep purples. I turned to Jay and flung my arms around his neck.

"Thank you," I whispered, kissing his lips.

"You're worth it and so much more," he whispered back into my lips.

"Ahem!" A very handsome man cleared his throat.

"Aiden! Meet Rox. Rox, meet Aiden," Jay introduced me to his brother.

"It's a pleasure to meet you, Rox. I've heard so many good things about you! And your Shizzle Sauce has won over so many of our customers! You are not only beautiful, but also very talented." His voice rolled off his tongue, just as sultry as Jay's. "Have a seat and relax! I'll be taking care of you tonight."

"Thank you, Aiden." I blushed.

That damn accent would be the death of me for sure. I'd never blushed until I heard the Aussies speak their sex talk.

I scooted into the middle of the booth, picking the perfect spot to oversee the dining room. Jay rushed in next to me and grabbed two menus from his brother, who quickly turned to go. The hostess, who was still standing there, handed me a black cloth napkin and a cocktail menu before leaving.

I looked from my napkin to Jay's white napkin. "Wow, black napkin for my dark dress. That's new. Never had anyone try to match my dress before. You really did think of everything with this place, didn't you?" I thumbed through the cocktail menu, nodding my head at every drink that sounded like nectar from heaven.

"They call me the restaurant whisperer. It's the little touches, like the color-coordinated napkins, that make people feel special and want to return. That is the goal. I want people to feel special and have an extraordinary experience when they eat here. I did that with all of our restaurants back home, and so far, it's worked well here too." He rested his hand on my leg, sending a jolt of fire throughout me and settling in between my thighs.

"Extraordinary indeed. Do you have a cocktail you recommend?"

"I do. It debuts tonight. It's called On the Rox. Terrance, our bartender, made it special for you. It's edgy with a bite but goes down smooth. But the real kicker on this cocktail is, it's our most beautiful one. The ice cube is frozen Shizzle Sauce, and the garnishment is Thai basil and a floating purple orchid blossom."

"Holy hell! Did you freeze Shizzle Sauce? And put it in a cocktail?"

"Its bite balances the sweetness, the gin binds it all together, and in the end, you have a mellow drink that will fuck you up quickly. It goes really fast." He laughed.

"I think this drink just became my new best friend. Can't wait to try it." I grinned.

A man named a drink after me? Fuck yes. He was speaking my language.

Aiden came back to take our orders and moved the gigantic bouquet so that we could people-watch. When Jay asked if I wanted the drapes closed or open, I said open for now. I liked to see how their restaurant operated. It almost made me want to open my own, except I could never put this together. My establishment would serve tacos, beer, and loud music. I stared out over the crowd, realizing how polar opposite Jay and I were. My mind only drifted for a moment before his brother popped right back over with our drinks and a tiny sample of something that looked like dirty toast.

"Amuse-bouche." Aiden set down a tiny plate in front of us both. "Vegemite on our in-house-made crouton. Sorry. Jay made me serve it to you." He shrugged.

"And here are your drinks," another man added, coming up behind Aiden and setting down two fancy glasses filled to the top with booze and a flower.

"Rox, this is Terrance, our creative genius of a bartender. He created your signature drink!" Jay smiled.

"Thank you, Terrance. It looks beautiful!" I smiled as both Terrance and Aiden grinned and tipped their heads, turning to leave us alone.

"So, this is On the Rox drink?" I asked, pulling my phone out and snapping a picture to send to the girls later. "I had to take a picture of that. It's gorgeous!"

"Like the woman it's named after. Try it. Then, try the Vegemite." Jay's eyes lit up brighter than the flickering candle in front of us.

I took a sip of the drink, the orchid topper gently nudging my lip, and rolled my eyes to the back of my head. It tasted like the nectar of the gods … or as I was sure Jay would say, goddess. Two more quick sips, and he was right. Already, my toes felt a tiny tingle.

"It's perfect, isn't it?" he said, taking a long, slow sip from his On the Rox cocktail too. "Like you."

"I'm hardly perfect. Watch, I won't like your Vegemite, and then you'll declare me a hard pass."

I picked up the buttery crouton and took a bite. It tasted like beef broth on toast. It wasn't bad at all. I had thought I would bite into a spreadable piece of ass, but I liked it.

"My bouche is amused!" I declared.

He fist-pumped the air before quickly getting his wits back about him and straightening his collar. I needed to tell him no one fist-pumped anymore, but I reveled in the moment of his joy. I felt it too. Everything was perfect, which was why I had to fuck it up. Chaos was familiar to me. Perfection was not.

"So, this treaty. I've run with you, been to your restaurant, and tried Vegemite. I'm three for three. You, on the other hand, are one for three. You only did Westy's with me. You still have the tattoo and poem. Where are you on those two? Didn't you say you had an idea on the tattoo?"

"Ah, right. I do. It's my cat's face. She died when I was seventeen, but I was very close to her. Still miss her. Here's her picture," he said, pulling out his phone and scrolling through his photos.

What the fuck?

I thought he was going to drop something deep on me, open up a bit more.

A damn cat tattoo? He could have at least picked something more badass, like a black panther or rabid tiger, but a cat?

I smiled politely, listening to his cat stories. Besides his sexy face and hot-as-hell body, it was his gentleness and kindness that attracted me to him. It would be out of character for him to tattoo a skull and bones across his chest. I could let his cat face slide.

"I think it's a brilliant idea. If that is what you want, that is what you should get. What about the poem?" I tilted my head to the side, sipping more of the On the Rox cocktail that made me brave. "Are you going to get deep into your feelings with your poem? Tell me about what goes on in that brilliant mind of yours."

"You're what goes on in this brilliant mind of mine." His jaw clenched as he swirled his drink and took a gulp.

"I mean, what do you want out of life? Why did you run from home, and do you plan on running again?" *There. I said it.* On the Rox had made me do it. I twisted the napkin under the table, waiting to hear if my future with him was impossible or not.

They always leave.

"What I want out of life is to settle down. I'm tired of running. I have no plans of ever doing that again. I've seen all I need to see. Now, I just want to live here and settle down. Rox, I don't want to scare you, but can I tell you something creepy?"

"I like creepy. Shoot!" The tension that left my body when he'd said he was staying and wanted to settle had me even more relaxed than the alcohol.

"My mother had a saying. She told my brother and me to stop chasing peacocks and to find the raven among them. She was an Outer Forks native. We were back and forth here, growing up, as we visited her side of the family often when I was younger. They are all gone now." His voice became low.

"I'm so sorry." I scooted myself even closer to him.

"No, no. It's fine. I just remembered the raven quote when I saw it on the back of your neck. It was an … otherworldly moment. I hope that doesn't make me sound crazy."

"Like divine intervention?"

"Yes. Exactly like divine intervention. Back to that again, are we? I've felt comfortable with you ever since. You're not like any woman I've ever met. I know you are still healing, and I'm so proud of all the work you have done to come out of a situation like you were in. You really are a goddess."

I noticed how he had turned the conversation back around to me.

"Thanks, Jay. You're doing amazing yourself! Look at this!" I waved my hand around the room, taking in his beautiful creation.

"Ah, that's nothing. Want to see what else I can do?" In one quick motion, he dived under the tablecloth.

"What are you doing?" My hand reached out to grab his arm as I tried to pull him back up.

He gently peeled my fingers off of him, kissing every one before setting my hand down on my lap.

"Eating my dessert before my dinner, like a bad boy," he growled from under the table.

I gasped but made no move to stop him.

"Where did Jay go?" Aiden came by the table.

I wanted to tell him to shut the drapes, but I didn't want to raise suspicion.

"Restroom, I think," I squeaked out as I felt Jay lift my dress.

His fingertips traced up and over my legs and in between my inner thighs. He pushed my knees apart.

"Okay. Well, we have a set menu tonight that he prepared especially for you. I'm sure he told you all about it. Would you like to make any changes?" Aiden asked.

I squirmed in my seat.

"Nope. No changes. I'm good. Real good." I nodded and even gave him a dorky thumbs-up.

"I'll be right back with a starter then." Aiden scuttled away just as I felt my panties being pulled to the side.

I hurried down in my chair and wiggled my hips into position as I slowly sipped my cocktail.

This is the life, I thought.

Jay's warm tongue slid all the way up my slit, stopping on my clit as he gently sucked it back into his mouth. I let out a gasp, startling us both as his head hit the underside of the table.

"Sorry! Sorry!" I whispered, leaning as far down as I could and talking to a table.

I sat back up, glancing around me and checking for curious eyes. No one had been paying attention, thankfully. I spread my legs apart further, signaling him to get back to it. With a cocktail in my hand and Jay's hair in the other, I sat back and let myself feel like royalty.

Here I was, a taco truck–owning rocker chick, sipping a cocktail named after me, in a white-tableclothed dining room with the most romantic man I'd ever met, who had his tongue on my pussy right under the table of the fancy restaurant he owned.

I'm so fucking lucky. Maybe divine intervention is real.

My breath became heavy as I finished my drink and grabbed the sides of the table. For someone who didn't like to go fast, Jay sure was working me down there. I wondered if he'd somehow snuck in a vibrator because, surely, his tongue couldn't be doing all that work. I groaned as he pushed a finger inside me.

"Jay still in the restroom?" Aiden's eyebrows rose into his hairline as my thighs tensed.

I stared stupefied like a deer in headlights—or like someone who had gotten caught having public sex.

"Uh, I think he had to take a call or something. I'm not sure. I'm okay though. Really, I am. I'll take another cocktail, if you don't mind. Thanks, Aiden." I winked. At least I didn't give him a thumbs-up this time.

Jay hummed between my thighs, vibrating the entire lower half of my body, as my feet began to twitch out from under me. I knew I was close and on the verge of something big when that occurred. My heel kicked the underside of the table as he motorboated me between my legs. My climax came on faster than I thought and right as Aiden reappeared again.

Damn it, I should have told him to close the curtain!

Waves of pleasure coursed through my body as my feet shot out to the sides and kicked under the table. I flew a foot off the booth and squealed.

"Ahh … sorry! My foot fell asleep! Tingles …" I breathed deep. "So … many tingles." My voice shook in what sounded like an attempt at a yodel.

"Would you like to walk it out? I can help you out of the booth and into some fresh air?" Aiden's brows were still raised into his hairline.

"No. Nope. I will just take this drink and forget about it. How's that food looking? I'm starving!" My clit throbbed hard, making my eyes bulge with each pulse. I was out of breath, and all I had done was sit back and enjoy my time. You'd think I'd run a marathon by the way I breathed.

"On it." He grinned.

My mouth fell open as he caught my gaze and winked before he closed the drapes.

"He's gone! You can come up now. And he knows!" I whispered under the table, lifting the skirt to see Jay come up for air.

His cheeks blushed red and were dewy … from me. That was hot as fuck.

"Well, it's not like he hasn't done anything like that before. He's wild, that one." Jay pressed his napkin to his face, drying off every bit of me and smiling.

"Still got an appetite, or are you satisfied now?" I put my arm around his waist and turned his chin with my finger, so he could kiss me. I tasted myself on his lips. I was his amuse-bouche. Fuck Vegemite.

"I'm insatiable for you. You taste like the nectar of the gods or the goddess." He stroked my hair out of my face and held me tight.

Nectar. Goddess.

I had been thinking about those things earlier.

How could he?

I felt the hard lump of rose quartz I'd hidden in my bra, much to Nikki's insistence. It lay heavy against my heart, tucked under my boob, and was growing warm.

NINE

Jay

I sat at my bar, tapping the pen to paper. My drink had become watered down by the time I even wrote one word of poetry.

I feel …

No, that's not right!

The night after our date at Scarlett Herb, Rox had invited me to drinks at her place. She'd shown me her collection of poems. Half of them were rip-your-heart-out tragic, and the other half of them were hilarious. She'd read aloud about everything from a heartbroken mess to a superhero to a premenopausal cat lady on the verge of a midlife crisis.

"Where do you get all of these ideas?" I asked. I rubbed a tear out of my eye. I wasn't sure if it had come from laughing so hard or the pain I felt in some of her words.

"From life." She kept flipping through her notebook, picking apart the poems she dared to read to me.

"I like the mixture you have. I've never thought about mixing the bad with the good. How does that work out?"

"You have to laugh to keep from crying sometimes. I get all the bad shit out, and I can also get all the silly shit out. That's supposed to cancel the bad shit. It doesn't really, but I think it knocks the edge off at least. It's a fine balance. It's a tactic we also use at the shelter. That's why poetry night can get a little crazy at The Lounge. You never know if you're about to laugh, cry, or as you like to do, fist pump."

"That's brilliant. Such a clever girl. Have you thought about publishing?"

"Yes. One day. When I get time. Business and volunteering have me too distracted right now to do much. You guys are selling my Shizzle Sauce faster than we can make it! I might have to get someone on that more than twice a week. Especially with the new cocktail you're using it in."

"That cocktail is an Instagram sensation. Our collaboration has been a hit." I fist-pumped the air, making her laugh.

"We make a good team." She closed her notebook and grabbed my hand.

"Yes, we do," I agreed, squeezing her hand.

We'd spent every night since date night at her place or mine.

I continued tapping my pen to the paper, grabbing a bar napkin and wiping up the condensation forming around my glass. I put my elbow on the counter and leaned my cheek into my palm, thinking. I could write about how she had the great idea to christen my home by doing it in every room.

I will fuck you in the yard.
I will fuck you oh-so hard.
I will fuck you on the chair.

I will fuck you over there.
I will fuck you anywhere.

Fuck! I suck.

"What in the bloody hell is this?" Aiden pulled up a barstool beside me, picked up my paper, and read aloud my words. "Are you writing poetry?"

"I'm trying to," I muttered, snatching my paper from him. "Think you can do better? Want to have a go, mate?" I waved the poem in front of his face.

"Actually, yeah, I do think so. Want me to try?"

"By all means." I held out my pen and sat back to watch my brother's competitive nature come out.

He jotted down a few lines and handed the paper back to me.

Your arse is a peach,
Gooey and sweet.
I'd put you on a pedestal
And grovel at your feet.

I read his work aloud, cringing.

"What the heck is that all about?" Nikki walked in with Layla trailing behind her right as I had spoken.

"Nothing! Nothing. It's nothing! Just ..." I shoved the paper in my coat pocket.

"I heard something about a gooey peach. And if my guess is right, you're trying to write poetry. If you ever use the word *gooey* when describing a woman, we're going to need to take you to an anatomy class." Nikki put a hand to her hip.

"Ew, yeah. Don't do that!" Layla's eyes fluttered as she sat down next to Aiden. "Juicy. It's juicy."

"I bet it is," Aiden growled. "I guess you're all here to make Shizzle, right? Betty called and scheduled the kitchen before the rush. Tell her thanks for that. Where is she anyway? Is she crewing the truck with Rox?"

"No, Rox got called out on some emergency at the shelter. She's operating the truck, but we have our stand-in employees working today." Nikki looked from me to Aiden. Her eyes were transfixed on both of us as if she was trying to read our thoughts. Knowing her, she probably was.

"Emergency? Is she okay?" My voice squealed. Then, I cleared my throat and said in a burly tone, "I mean, is she safe?"

"She's fine. I'm sure she will text you the first chance she gets." Nikki twirled her crystal necklace between her fingers.

"Come on. Let's get down to business and make this sauce." Layla clutched Nikki's elbow and pulled her toward the back.

"Right this way, ladies!" Aiden motioned for them to follow.

"I'll be right there!" Nikki called after them while still staring a hole straight through me.

A mild sense of panic arose in me as I thought for a brief moment that she might perhaps be reading my thoughts. It wasn't like I was thinking anything dirty.

Rox, Rox, Rox.
Safe.
Boobs.
Shit!
Fucking Rox in the boobs!
Fuck!
Why can't my brain stop?
Nikki's going to think I'm a perv!
Baseball.
Soccer.
Boring old men in the sauna.
Ew.
Boobs!

I wiped a beat of sweat from my brow.

"Are you okay?" Nikki smirked.

"Yep. Fine. It's been a rush today. Now about to get prepped for the dinner crowd." I fumbled with my pen, unable to look back up at her mind-reading eyes.

"If you're writing a poem for Rox, just a wild guess here"—she winked—"might I suggest that you write about your feelings. Why you ran away from home maybe? You can probably relate to her on that level of brokenness. Because she thinks you're a god, and I know you think she is a goddess. She is. And maybe you are too. But everyone is fucked up. It's good to not be alone in it. I think your perfection might make her feel inferior."

"What? She said that?" I sat my pen down, feeling dizzy. "I'd never want her to feel that way at all."

"She probably feels lots of ways because she is still healing. And I think you are too. I know she mentioned you traveled the world after some family accident. Write about it. Tell her about it. Relate to her on that level. Heal together. It's not exactly rocket science that you bumped into each other and you're both healing."

"Why do you think I'm still healing?"

"I can see it in your eyes."

I quickly looked down. "Damn it! I knew you were a mind reader!"

Rox.

Sex.

Soccer.

Rox.

Arse and titties.

Fuck!

"I'm not a mind reader." She laughed. "You can look up at me! I can't read your dirty thoughts about boobs. No worries."

I gasped, feeling my heart plummet down into my testicles.

"Lucky guess! You're a man. Come on now!" She put her hand on my shoulder and gave it a shake. "Listen, I'm trying to help you, and I'm trying to help my best friend.

I'm going about it different than Betty, so be grateful. I'll not cut you up into crocodile boots. I'll put a spell on you that makes you wish you were a pair of crocodile boots."

My head began to swim as I glanced up and toward the exit.

"I can't catch a break with DTF." I rubbed my hands over my face.

"No one can. Just do the damn thing I told you to do. Take advantage of the divine intervention that came shooting down and hooked you two up together. Even if it's only for a short while."

"What do you mean, a short while?" My heartbeat pulsed loud in my ears.

Does she know something I don't?

"I mean, no one knows the future." She shrugged, walking away toward the kitchen.

Except you.

Balls.

Boobs.

Rox.

Rox and I had barely seen each other over the last few days. Her job and volunteer work had kept her busy, and Scarlett Herb's customers had increased twofold since teaming up with The Pink Taco Truck. Suddenly, our doors were graced with hipsters, yogis, and college-aged kids looking for Shizzle cocktails and trying out our locally sustained farm-to-table menu. Nikki had told me she was in charge of social media for the taco truck, and lately, she'd been giving Scarlett Herb shout-outs. I didn't know much about shout-outs, but whatever they were had been working.

No longer did Scarlett Herb sport the tired, older generation's faces sniffing their brandy and growling over their bills. Our image was slowly changing into the *it* place. We became much more modern artsy than old-fart stuffy, which was what Aiden had said he wanted all along. Even though I had consulted and made a few changes here and there, I felt Rox and DTF were responsible for a lot of our business. Old man Earl had even become a regular customer of ours.

I lay in my bed, laptop open, going over invoices and spreadsheets. I needed to thank Rox in some way. She worked so damn hard, and now, I was reaping her benefits too. I took a break from work and scoured the internet for some type of gift I thought she might like. She didn't seem the kind of woman to care for jewelry, and I thought it was still too early to surprise her with a getaway.

Unless we went back to Westy's.

No. It needs to be something more.

I heard her car door slam next door, startling me out of my tired state of mind. My phone buzzed beside me.

> *Rox: Still up?*

> *Me: Yep. Can't sleep. How was your night? I was worried about you. It's after one!*

> *Rox: You don't have to worry about me. My night was the same as usual. Rough. But I think we are getting closer to getting the new family settled. So, hopefully, next week, things will slow down in that part of my life.*

> *Me: Good! I would love some more nights with you. Would you like a lullaby to send you off to sleep? Or maybe some more dirty instructions?*

Rox: I'll take a warm body. Is it too late for that? We live right next door to each other and yet rarely see each other.

Me: Putting on my thongs and coming. Be right there!

Rox flung the door open before I could knock.

"Where are these thongs? That is hot as fuck! Take your pants off and turn around! I want to see!" She clasped her hands together, bouncing on her toes.

"Um, these?" I stuck my foot out, showing her my footwear.

The weather had become increasingly hot over the last week, which meant I'd needed to buy summer clothes. A quick trip to the shops had resulted in a brand-new wardrobe, thongs included.

"Not your flip-flops! Your thongs! You said you were wearing some over." Her mouth turned down into a pout.

"Oh! No, we call flip-flops thongs! I'm so sorry! I'm afraid I don't have any thongs. But if that is what you like, I'll get a pair tomorrow!"

"Want to borrow mine?" She lifted her skirt and turned her back toward me, bending over and showing me the thin black string that disappeared into her arse.

"Fuck. I'll do whatever you want!"

I stepped inside, and with one quick motion, I swept her off her feet and into my arms. She threw her hands around my neck and puckered her lips.

"Kiss me! I missed you! We need to get better schedules!"

I nibbled her lips, too busy to respond with anything other than an, "Mmhmm."

"Let's go upstairs. I need some Jay time," she mumbled into my mouth.

Her breaths were soft and minty against my lips. I pulled her tightly into me, squeezing her and breathing in the scent of her neck. She smelled divine—nectar of the goddess.

"I want to feel you wrapped around me, clinging to me that moment I first enter you, your sweet pussy gripping around my cock. I need to feel that. And I want you to tell me if you can feel my heartbeat pulsing inside of you."

Her chest rose up, poking her perfectly round breasts closer to my face, as if pleading for me to take them in my mouth right here. We stood in the doorway, unable to tear our eyes off each other.

"That's the hottest thing I've ever heard. Fuck!" She sucked in her lower lip between her teeth, biting it.

"*You're* the hottest thing ever, Kintsugi," I growled into her ear, kicking the door shut behind me before gently setting her down.

She started undressing while walking up the stairs, flinging her clothes left and right. Her shirt ended up in the hall, one of her shoes landed on the kitchen table, her bra caught on the railing of the stairs. I followed suit behind her although much less graceful. My thongs knocked an empty cup over, and I had to hop on one foot to wiggle out of my underwear. I fumbled with the buttons on my pajama shirt while she slipped her thongs off, swirled them around her index finger in the air, and threw them at me. They landed directly at my feet.

My heart beat in my chest, matching the rhythm of my throbbing cock. I picked her knickers up off the floor and breathed them in while she watched. I had no idea what I was doing at the moment. I needed her scent on me—all over me. I wanted to wear her like cologne. I let out a low, rumbling growl that even scared me a little and tore the buttons off my shirt.

"Oh my! You're just … you're… what do y'all say? Bloody hell!" she said, her chest rising and falling at the same rhythm as my pulse. "The last one to bed is a rotten fart barn!" She ran up the stairs, chased by whatever beast had come out in me, which I would like to think was much more lion and much less wallaby. But for some reason, only a wallaby came to mind.

I caught up with her as she dived into bed, giggling as I crawled my way on top of her. My dick acted like a honing device as I felt the tip search out her wet pussy, nudging her until it slid right into home. That was what she felt like—home. Her hands reached up to my cheeks, pulling my mouth down to hers. I was two seconds away from going to pound town when she locked her legs over my hips and stopped me from moving.

"I want it slow. Can we do that? Like you said. I want to feel your heartbeat inside of me." A shy smile played across her lips as she cast her eyes down.

I'd never seen this badass babe bashful before, and I'd never seen her want to do anything slow either. I kissed the tip of her nose.

"Your pleasure is my pleasure," I whispered as I slowly thrust inside her, making love to her.

I woke in the middle of the night, sitting up in the dark to get my bearings. I smoothed the sheets next to me, realizing I sat in an empty bed. My heart jumped as I still assumed that Rox wasn't okay. Half-asleep, I slipped a sheet around me and stumbled around the room, finding my way down the dark stairs and toward the light of the kitchen.

"Hey there. I hope I didn't wake you." Rox sat at a table with her feet propped up on a chair, completely naked and eating cheesecake.

"No, I thought something was wrong. That's all. Sorry, I'm still half-asleep." I pulled up a chair beside her, grinning at the sight of crumbs falling down her bare chest.

"Want some cheesecake? It's my comfort food. Sometimes, when I can't sleep at night, I wake up, eat cheesecake, write poetry," she said, holding up her fork and notebook.

"Comfort food? Is everything okay? I had a lovely night. Did something go wrong?"

"No. Not at all! Everything was perfect! I have a rattled brain still from all the stress of this week. I needed to pour it out on paper."

"I see. Well, how about I make you what my mum used to make me on bad nights? We have our own version of comfort food in Australia. It's called fairy bread."

"That sounds interesting. What's in it?"

"Bread, butter, and hundreds and thousands. That's what we call sprinkles. I can run to my house and get it. Can I make you some?"

"I have all of that here! Have at it. Butter in the fridge, bread, and sprinkles—I mean, hundreds and thousands—in the pantry." She nodded toward an open door in her kitchen.

I arose to my feet, flung the sheet off of me, and made myself comfortable, much to her laughter.

"What? Can't a man make some fairy bread while naked in his neighbor's kitchen just before dawn?"

"You can do anything naked in my kitchen or anywhere. Keep going. You're giving me ideas." She scribbled into her notebook, pausing to look up at me before writing down more words.

I gathered my ingredients and washed my hands. The cold water splashed on my bare abs, sending a chill straight down to my willy. It shrank into hiding. I turned my hips away from Rox, hoping she hadn't noticed my poor little fellow, but the giggles I heard told me otherwise.

"Ahem," I cleared my throat. "An Australian masterpiece is coming right up!" I announced as I spread butter across the bread and trimmed the crusts. I sliced it into triangles and generously decorated it with hundreds and thousands.

"You are an Australian masterpiece. With a body like that. You look like you've been carved out of stone." She held her pen to her mouth, nibbling on the end.

"Thank you. You know I did see the statue of *David* in Florence. It was magnificent. Everything in Italy is magnificent." I sat the plate of fairy bread in front of her.

"Carbs and sugar! You get me. Tell me more about your travels." She picked up a piece of the bread and nibbled it, the hundreds and thousands falling onto her naked breasts.

I reached out, picking them off one by one and popping them into my mouth. "I've been all over the place. What would you like to hear?"

She licked her lips and pushed her plate of cheesecake toward me. "You eat that, and I'll eat this. Living the life!" She laughed. "Hmm … I don't know too much about history. Tell me what gave you the most feels when you saw it."

"That one is easy. But it gives me the feels now more than when I saw it. Although when I saw it, I was awestruck too."

"Go on," she said, brushing the crumbs off of her hands and onto the plate and smacking her lips.

"Sistine Chapel. Specifically, *The Creation of Adam*. Do you know that famous part of the chapel where God is reaching out his hand to touch Adam's? God's finger is straight and full of life, and Adam's is just hanging there, limp, lifeless. That's how I feel now with you. There's not any other way to explain it. I feel like you touch me and bring me to life. You awaken my mind, my body, my soul."

"You're going to nail this poetry thing." She shook her head as if trying to shake off the pink that had crept across her cheeks.

"Maybe. You're making it easier for me to find my words." I grabbed the sheet and wrapped it around myself, holding it open. "Come on. Let's watch the sunrise. I'm going to wrap you up and keep you snuggled safely next to me."

She pressed herself against me, nuzzling her head under my chin. The tension from her body melted away as soon as I closed the sheet around us.

"Jay?" Her voice came out quiet and shaking.

"Hmm?"

"Thanks for calming me and comforting me and just being you. I'm so glad to have you in my life. I feel so lucky."

"Me too, Kintsugi. Me too."

TEN

Rox

Work at the shelter and with the taco truck had overwhelmed me to the point of exhaustion. Lucky for me, I had a new man who picked me up when I felt down and comforted me when I needed it—which was always. During the day, I would receive random text messages of audio recordings that ranged anywhere from happy pick-me-up songs sang in his sexy accent to dirty-talking recordings of what he would like to do to me the next chance he saw me.

I giggled my way through food prep. Betty and Nikki seemed skeptical of my new, bubbly mood, but Layla was amused.

"It's magic! I can see that sparkle in your eyes! Nikki's stones, they work! I put one in my panties last night, and I can't say it was comfortable, but I finally got laid!" Layla clasped her hands together as if a prayer had been answered.

"By Aiden?" I asked.

"Heavens no! Some random dude at The Lounge! Aiden and I aren't a thing. We're just friends. Flirty friends." Layla rolled her eyes.

"Friends? Yeah, right! You two seemed a lot flirtier than just friends. I can barely keep you two from drooling on each other when we're making Shizzle Sauce!" Nikki interjected, shaking her head in disbelief. "Friends!" She laughed.

"I don't get what's so funny! Haven't you had a friend you can get all flirty with without the commitment?" Layla asked.

"Since when have you not wanted the commitment? You've been planning a wedding since you were five." Betty tapped her spatula on the side of the pan and side-eyed Layla.

"My wedding will have to wait for the right man. I don't get the feeling that Aiden likes me like that. He flirts and all, but his eyes aren't all puppy dog when he sees me. He looks happy enough to eat me up. And only eat me up. Not wife me up." Layla sighed. "Forever a bridesmaid, never a bride."

"You'll still be the first to get married, Layla." Nikki laughed. "I don't think any of us are even close."

"Hell no!" Betty smacked her spatula down hard onto the countertop. "Every woman in my family who has gotten married has also gotten divorced. Sometimes, two or three times. My aunt divorced four times! She has sworn off men and is now a full-on lesbian. I don't blame her. I haven't met one worth all the trouble they give."

"What if they give you no trouble?" I asked, unhinging the back door to hop out and set up tables before officially opening the truck to taco orders.

"Then, you're dating a woman! That's not a man, but a woman! I can guarantee, they are less trouble. Ask Nikki," Betty said.

"Oh jeez! It was only a short fling. And, yes, it was worth every second of it. But I'm addicted to peen. My lesbian days are over. Too bad she moved away. I enjoyed my time with her. I can say that women do make amazing lovers. I haven't met anyone as thoughtful and romantic since." Nikki sat her prepped food aside and climbed out of the truck to help me.

We gathered the tables out of the back of Layla's van and began to set up shop. We were parked outside of a corporate park today, which meant we would sell out to customers who huffed down our tacos, all while conducting business meetings on their phones, too busy to interact with us. DTF let it roll off of our backs. We were all thankful we didn't lead that type of life even if it would pay the bills more easily than what we were doing.

"How's The Steamy Clam gig? Still paying off?" I asked Nikki while we walked back and forth, setting up seating.

"It is! I love it! I was going to see if you and the girls wanted to come out to my official debut as a Steamy Clam dancer! They want me as a regular on their weekends and during some weeknights. I told them to let me get some time to work out a routine. So, I'm thinking maybe two weeks from now, I'll officially be part of their team and not just some part-time fill-in amateur." Nikki bounced on her heels.

"Oh my gosh! That is amazing! Of course I'll be there. I am so proud of you! I can't wait to see what you come up with! Have you figured out your stage name yet?" I asked.

"Crystal Cream Pie. Crystal because, duh, but Cream Pie because I have this thing I've been doing with cream pies. The men love it. I love it. What's not to love?"

"I think DTF will love it too! Can't wait to see you perform!" I put my arms around Nikki's neck and squeezed her tight.

To see the smile on her face when she talked about dancing made my day even brighter. Things were looking up for all of us. I wasn't sure if it was from Nikki's crystals or us growing older and more comfortable in our skin or because the worst of our lives were now past us. We had all dealt with enough shit to last a lifetime.

My phone buzzed in my back pocket, sending me into an even wider smile.

"Better get that." Nikki winked. "Any man who can make you smile like that might just be comparable to a woman."

I nodded in agreement, ducking away to take Jay's call.

"I didn't want anything, except to hear your voice and tell you that you're beautiful. I know we're both busy, so I'll keep it short. You're the most gorgeous woman I've ever laid eyes on, and just the thought of you makes my knees buckle and my brain swim. I want to breathe you in, holding you in my lungs until I'm dizzy with the scent of you. Knowing that I've done that before and you're still in my bloodstream makes me the luckiest man alive. Hope you have an amazing day, sunshine."

I could barely catch my breath long enough to sigh into the phone, "Fuck! You're good!" and tell him good-bye.

I was much less eloquent, but I figured he understood I felt the same as him. I slid my phone back into my pocket and turned our sign around to read *Open*, much to our line's approval. I counted twelve people in front already, and we were just getting started.

The lunch hours passed by quick and busy, as usual. When we finally hit a slow point, we packed up and moved to our dinner location a few blocks away, near a music festival that was happening in a local park. We set up shop alongside other food trucks and started a quick prep before opening yet again to another hungry line of customers.

I didn't mind the fast-paced business that came with what we were doing. Especially when my work office was inside The Pink Taco Truck at a music festival in a beautiful park, surrounded by amazing people. I looked out over the crowd toward the stage as I prepared orders. I watched as hoopers performed tricks, babies danced on picnic blankets, and teenagers laughed in their groups. My life had come full circle.

This time, not very long ago, I wouldn't have noticed any of these things. My mind would have been too spastic to focus on anything, except for my problems and my easy waitress job back at the diner. And now, Betty had come into my life and Nikki and Layla and Earl—who I wouldn't even have the taco truck without. I couldn't imagine a better life for me. The icing on the cake was the new man in my life who seemed to have shown up out of nowhere, as if he had fallen from the sky.

The stars are aligning. I tried to shake the thought from my head even though the idea of it was beginning to grow on me.

Jay had done more for me in the short while that he had known me than any man had ever done for me. I felt good about myself with him—confident. He had lifted me and not once dragged me down. I knew he had struggled with his past just as I struggled with mine, so maybe I was his divine help for him too.

"I'm going to take a fifteen-minute break!" I told the girls as I hurried off to the front of the stage.

I wanted to get a closer look at the band and feel the music in my soul. I needed to file this moment in my memory bank because everything was right in the world, and this was what I had been striving for all of my life.

I wedged myself into the middle of the crowd, tossed my hair behind my shoulders, and swayed my hips to the music. I closed my eyes, feeling the beat pulse through my veins when I felt a body push up against me. I quickly turned around to Betty's laughter. She held her hand out to dance with me as Layla and Nikki followed behind.

We all held hands, dancing in a circle and rolling our bodies to the music. I watched Nikki as she gyrated. I wouldn't be surprised if she tore her shirt off and shook her boobs around. The thought of that made me laugh, which triggered a reaction to all the girls—a circle of laughter.

We were witches casting a spell of love and laughs out into the world. No more toxic bullshit! That was the spell. No drama. No negative energy. I'd hang a crystal on everything I owned and smudge myself every morning to continue feeling like this.

I shook my hair out, running my fingertips along my scalp to quiet my brain that had begun to be a buzzkill, bringing up what-if scenarios.

If things felt too good to be true, they usually were.

The brief moment of clarity killed my smile, but I didn't stop dancing.

I pulled up to my house a little after three a.m., already planning on calling Betty in the morning to tell her that I couldn't make it in today and to call in a stand-in employee if she needed it. Tonight had been the worst of the worst.

When the caseworker at the shelter had called me as we were closing up shop, I had a terrible feeling of dread wash over me. She told me that two new families came into the shelter, requiring immediate attention. She needed me and my skills there. She'd told me once a while back that I was relatable. She had urged me to tell survivors my story and comfort them with my whole *been there, done that* lifestyle.

I hated talking about it, but the more I talked about it, the easier it became for me to accept it. And helping others through situations I was familiar with made me feel more fulfilled than anything I'd ever done in life.

So, when I got the call to come and work my magic on the new families arriving this evening, I did everything in my power to get there and lighten their moods as much as I was able.

It worked too. I had gotten a few smiles out of the moms and quite a lot more out of the children.

If The Pink Taco Truck hadn't worked out, I would have loved to get my degree in social work and do this sort of thing for a living.

I slammed my car door shut, noticing Jay's light still on upstairs. A pang of guilt flashed through my chest as I realized he was probably waiting up on me. I stopped at my front door, pausing to reflect on that feeling. I didn't want him to wait up for me. I didn't want to feel like I had to be home at a specific time so that he could sleep. I didn't want to feel tied down or controlled in that way.

Where is this coming from?

I pushed that annoying thought into the back of my head and dragged my feet inside. My eyes burned with exhaustion. I couldn't wait for the morning, so I could tell Jay all about how I'd helped the new families and made them laugh. I had even shared some poetry with the kids and encouraged them to write their own. He would be proud, and maybe it would be the nudge to get him to write that damn poem he had promised to write as part of the treaty.

My phone buzzed, startling me out of my drowsy state as I readied myself for bed.

> *Jay: Are you okay? Where have you been?*

I scanned the text four times, rubbing my eyes to make sure I'd read that right. My heartbeat began to quicken as an icky feeling overcame me. This situation was all too familiar.

> *Me: I've been at the shelter. Of course I'm okay. Why are you up so late?*

Jay: I wish you would text me when you're going to be gone all night. I got worried about you! I didn't know if you were in a wreck or something had happened.

Like what? Am I at another man's house or something?

My brain immediately thought of the scenarios Tommy had always accused me of doing. I could be out buying shampoo, and Tommy would have told me I was fucking his best friend. I would never fuck his best friend. He had a beer gut the size of a keg and breath that smelled like rotted eel. I swallowed hard before texting Jay back.

Me: I am fine. No need to worry about me. I can take care of myself.

I began to grow annoyed. I was too tired to justify myself, and really, why the fuck was I explaining myself? I was a twenty-nine-year-old woman busting my ass, taking care of everyone, and I was proud of myself tonight. But now? Now, I felt pissed. The other night, Jay had left me feeling serene and calm, but tonight, the familiar dread that I'd felt with Tommy had risen in my chest the second my phone buzzed.

Jay: Okay. I worry, is all. I had a nightmare and thought maybe you weren't okay. We can talk about it tomorrow.

Me: There's nothing to talk about. I worked late. Are you okay? Are you worried I am with someone else or something?

Jay: No! Were you?

Me: You're right. We can talk about this tomorrow. I'm tired. I worked my ass off too hard to deal with drama tonight.

I shut my phone off and slid into bed. I stopped myself from turning it back on to check his last words several times. In just a few short minutes, my night and my thoughts of Jay had been the polar opposite of what I had felt previously. I tossed and turned in bed, tired as hell, but my mind wouldn't stop thinking back to the text that had triggered me. I realized being asked questions was a trigger for me that I needed to work on, thanks to my asshole ex-boyfriend, Tommy. But I hadn't expected Jay to trigger me like that. Things had been going right, and he'd flipped out—or I'd flipped out. I was too confused and too tired for this.

I tried to take his past into account. The past that he still hadn't told me much about.

How can I see things from his point of view if he never opens up about it?

I shook the thoughts from my head and squeezed my eyes shut tight, forcing myself to sleep. I could handle this tomorrow. I didn't like the feeling I had, and after all I had been through, I never wanted to feel like this again.

"Betty?" I croaked into the phone. "Please call one of the other employees to fill in for me today. I've gotten exactly forty-five minutes of sleep."

"What? Why? Shelter troubles or man troubles?"

"Both." I squeezed the bridge of my nose.

"Okay. It looks like a new Crocodile Dundee–skinned purse for me. If you hear some screams from next door, just turn some music up and pretend you didn't."

"No, no. It's nothing like that. I stayed up late at the shelter, and Jay kind of freaked out when I didn't come home until this morning. I got in around three, and he was still waiting up for me. I don't know if my feelings of being annoyed are valid or not. Am I annoyed just because Tommy used to monitor me? Or should I be happy Jay is concerned about my well-being? I don't know, and I can't figure it out right now. I'm too tired, and the shelter wore me down already."

"Listen, your feelings are valid, no matter what. Whatever you are feeling, that's all you. It's not right or wrong. You've been in some bad situations, and you are reacting in the way you know how. I knew you were still healing your scars when he came along. I hoped he could help you along the way. I'm not telling you what to do or not do. You know that. You know I support you in whatever decision you make. But maybe slow down and focus on yourself. Stop taking care of everyone else. Take tomorrow off too. We got the truck. Also, tell the shelter you need a break, okay? You need a few mental health days to figure it out and then slowly start getting back to the grind."

"How come you are so smart?"

"I watched my mama go through this shit. You know that! It's going to take a long, long time. I doubt Jay meant anything by it. Honestly, the man seems like he couldn't hurt a flea if he wanted to. But we aren't focusing on him. We're focusing on you. Text me anytime you need me. I'll check back in later. Get some sleep and worry about the situation when you're rested. I love you."

"Love you too, Betty. Thanks. Tell the girls I'm fine too, please. Don't need anyone else worrying."

I hung up my phone and pulled the covers up over my head. Tommy had manipulated my mind into confusion for years. The counselors at the shelter had helped me somewhat, but I also struggled with taking the time to know myself—and most importantly, trust myself. I bit my lip hard, tasting metallic.

Trust myself. My feelings are valid.

Since Jay's restaurant didn't open until eleven, I knew he hadn't yet left for work when I woke back up at nine. I touched my fingertips to my puffy eyes and groaned. I needed more sleep, but I also needed to handle this situation, or it would eat me alive. These words needed to come out and not on paper this time. Yesterday, I'd had a feeling when I was happy and content with life that things would come crashing down. I'd thought I had moved past the trauma in my life, but I still had work to do.

I called Jay to make sure he was home and available to chat.

"Good morning," I said. "Are you home?"

"Good morning, sunshine! I just got home from a late run. What's up? Everything okay?" He breathed heavy into the phone.

"I was going to stop by for a quick chat. I've had something on my mind since last night."

"Oh. Last night. Yes." His voice fell flat. "I'm here."

"In person. I'm walking over now. Talk soon."

I slipped on my house shoes and dragged my feet down the stairs. My pajamas were green with the Slytherin emblem decorated all over, but I didn't care how juvenile I looked. Jay wouldn't mind. He didn't mind at all who I was as a person. He liked my odd quirks and wild, over-the-top shenanigans. And that was what made walking up to his home difficult. I needed to understand last night's actions and put the brakes on what would inevitably turn into just another one of my disasters.

I stepped up to his door, noticing that he kept the blinds shut and remembering the morning I'd caught him spewing his load all over the place. I giggled to myself, trying to focus on something funny and pushing down the pain that had settled into my heart. I was still beginning to figure myself out, but I knew this much was true. I wasn't ready to commit to anyone or anything. Not after a simple, caring question had set me off.

He opened the door before I could knock and immediately pulled me into an embrace. I nuzzled my favorite spot against his chest for a quick second to feel his warmth before I pulled back and looked up at him.

I gritted my teeth, took a deep breath, and began, "Last night, when you freaked out on me, I didn't like that. I know you were coming from a different place than my ex, Tommy, but it still made me feel triggered." I folded my arms across my chest, the lump in my throat growing bigger and bigger. I wondered just how long I could swallow the wail that I knew was coming.

"Rox, I am so, so sorry. Please believe me. I would never be that type of man. That just isn't me, and I think you know that. I awoke in a panic from a horrible dream. It was of you. I reacted poorly. I did freak out. I wasn't even coherent when I woke. I feel terrible about that. Since my parents' accident, I'm afraid to lose someone else I love."

"What did you just say?" My stomach turned.

His admittance brought a whole new level of drama to the conversation I'd forced myself to have with him. I felt sick.

"I ... I love you, and I don't want to lose you. I worry about you. Too much. I know you're an independent woman. I want to keep you safe. From everyone. And everything. And if you're not feeling safe with me, then I will back off too. The last thing I want is to make you feel bad. I'll not have that. It was a misunderstanding, but I know where you are coming from. I understand. I really do." He buried his face in his hands and then ran his fingers through his hair. His mouth turned down into a pout, and the look in his eyes told me that he had already beaten himself up over this.

I had never seen him like this before. My pulse raced throughout my fingertips as I ached to reach out to him and forget the way I had felt last night.

"I'm sorry, Jay. I need some time. I told you, I'm broken. I don't know how to trust, and I don't know how to be in a healthy relationship. I'm trying, but I am a very slow work in progress. I can't help how I reacted either. It was a natural instinct for me. But my feelings are valid even if they were coming from a misunderstanding. I need to work on that. I'm not *kintsugi*. There is no gold here. It's only darkness, confusion, and walls that I've got to keep from crumbling for the wrong people."

"You think I'm the wrong people?" The hurt in his voice felt like a jab to my heart.

"No. I thought we'd met at the right time in each other's lives. Divine intervention and all that jazz. But maybe it is the wrong time. I'm still not healed, and neither are you. I need some time. That's all I'm saying."

"Okay. But I want you to know that you don't have to be so tough all the time. It's okay to lean on someone else for help. It's okay to be vulnerable and open and let someone take care of you for a change."

"You don't have to be so tough all the time either. You've not exactly opened yourself up to me, as I have to you. I know you're hurt and healing too. Even though our circumstances are different, we are still both at low points in our lives," I said, blinking back the tears that began to sting my eyes. "I have to go." I turned to run back toward home.

"Wait!" he called out after me after I already made it halfway across his yard. "Take all the time you need. Whether you like it or not, you are *kintsugi*. I look at you, and I only see golden rays. Sunshine. You're sunshine to my storms. I'm sorry for any pain I caused, Rox."

I dragged myself inside of my house, not turning back to catch his eyes that I'd felt staring at me the entire time I walked back home. I put my forehead to a wall, collapsing into a puddle on the cold hardwood floor. I wondered if I would ever be normal enough for a relationship again.

ELEVEN

Jay

Crushed didn't begin to explain how I felt after Rox left. I watched her as she walked away and back into her home, knowing that she wouldn't be coming back for a while, if ever. I closed my front door and sat on my couch in silence for over an hour. My chest hurt with that empty feeling that only came from a broken heart. I had been afraid to lose Rox, and because of that fear, I had lost her.

I put my head in my hands and thought back to that last week in Australia when I had fled my country days after my parents' funeral. I had taken no time in grieving. That shit wasn't for me. I had picked up and left, letting Aiden handle my affairs and accounts. It was a selfish thing to do, and I would be forever grateful to Aiden for taking care of business, but the shock of my divorce and my parents' deaths had me fly away in my own way. And now, I was stuck in a perpetual state of fear of loss because I never dealt with my shit.

I lay down on my couch, pulling the throw over on me and wrapping myself up. For the rest of the week, I let myself grieve.

TWELVE

Jay

Five Weeks Later

Ever since Rox had told me that she needed to slow things down, my days began to run together. I worked morning, noon, and night at Scarlett Herb to keep my mind off of my raven that needed to spread her wings and fly away. She was right in that I wasn't able to completely open up. I knew that for sure. I also knew that I needed closure myself. My own running away around the entire world hadn't helped me one bit.

I laced up my runners and quietly made my way outside as the sun rose over the hills. I looked up at Rox's window, knowing she probably still slept soundly this morning. We had successfully avoided each other since she showed up on my doorstep that morning weeks ago, but I would give anything to see her face again. I sighed. The heavy fog dampened my pants, reminding me of that time

I had taken Rox for a run and that rabid squirrel attacked me.

Bloody monster!

I pressed my heels into the muddy path and took off, hoping I didn't see another one of those bastards again. I could still feel Rox's breath on my neck as I pushed her up against that tree. That had been my first and last run with her. Unfortunately, my good habits hadn't rubbed off on her, but I had caught her another time or two eating fairy bread.

Like a dumbass, I never held up my entire end of the treaty with Rox. I hadn't been able to get my cat tattoo, and I never finished my poem. But now, it was too late. Rox didn't want to hear from me, and I wasn't going to be the person to push myself on her. I had a feeling she had enough pushing around in her life. If she really wanted me and our meeting really had been something out of the cosmos, she and I would be together again at some point. Maybe that wasn't now or anytime soon. But if it was meant to be, it would be.

I swallowed hard, stopping in the middle of my run and breathing the damp air into my lungs. I rubbed the tears out of my eyes. It was meant to be. I knew it was meant to be. Just like my parents had been soul mates, I had felt that with Rox. I had known her for a million years. My soul had known her. The thought of letting go of someone who touched your whole being like that crushed me. She had taught me to live when death had consumed my life.

I cut my run short and headed toward home, finally realizing what I needed to do. I never wanted to scare Rox away again. At least, while I gave her the space she had asked for, I could be the person I needed to be for me. Even though I felt she had helped me to be that person, it wasn't fair of me to ask her to do that. She already had enough people to help in her life.

I skipped my shower and headed into work straightaway after my run. I had mud caked to my shins, and I smelled like a bear, but I needed to get to DTF while they were using our kitchen. I knew they were there early every Monday and Thursday mornings because I'd successfully avoided running into them, too, these last few weeks. But today, I needed to talk to them even though the thought of seeing Betty after Rox and I had split seemed downright terrifying.

I pulled into the parking lot, noticing that The Pink Taco Truck was already there. I grabbed my keys and headed inside, busting through the door like the Kool-Aid Man and startling everyone. The restaurant wasn't set to open for another few hours, so it was only employees who saw me in my disheveled state.

"Wow, this breakup has hit you pretty bad, hasn't it?" Nikki said as she stared at me, wide-eyed.

"What? Oh. No. Well, yes actually. Never mind that. I was running and—" I searched around the room, finally seeing Betty at the back in deep conversation with Terrance.

I jogged over to them both, trying to control my breathing and not look like the complete mess I was.

"Hey! I have a favor to ask of you. Can I talk to you in private for a minute?" I wrapped my fingers around Betty's elbow and gently nudged her to the side.

Betty's eyes glanced from my grip on her elbow to my eyes. "Look, the only reason I haven't skinned you alive right now is because I know that it wasn't your fault. Even though she is upset, it's with herself, not you. But I do want to take it out on you, just so you know. I don't know why. Maybe I got some deep-shit issues too. But shoot, what were you saying?" Betty put her hands on her hips and squinted at me.

I thought I'd seen this stance before from a deadly bird-o-saurus back home in the outback.

"I wanted to know if you thought it would be okay if I read Rox's poetry. She mentioned she wanted it published one day, so I think she would be okay with me reading it all, but I want you to make sure for me and see if maybe I can borrow it for my own healing. You can tell her that. I find it—her—inspirational. I want to read more of her work. Please ask her if she can let me borrow that notebook," I pleaded, noticing Betty's posture relax as she took a deep breath.

"She'd love nothing more than to help. You know that about her. I'll get it to you."

"How has she been? Okay?" My eyes searched Betty's for any clue as to if Rox had been safe, comfortable, happy, and maybe even if she had thought about me at all.

"Don't push it." Betty grabbed her boobs, pushed them up to her neck, and then pulled her palms away, letting them fall into a bounce.

I didn't know if I was more scared or turned on.

"Um, was that some type of Bat-Signal? Is that an American gesture? Like a handshake?" I put my palms to my chest and rubbed my pecs up and down.

"Boob drop. Like a mic drop, except by me. So, ten times the impact. Now, I've got to get to work. Will get you those poems, Kangaroo Boy!" she said, turning on her heels to leave.

Crocodile Dundee was a much cooler nickname.

Nikki stopped me as I made my way to the exit.

"Take this. Keep it in your shirt pocket. Close to that broken heart of yours," she said, sliding a pink crystal into my palm.

"Thanks, Nikki." I pocketed the smooth stone and walked back to my car, ready to tackle the rest of my life.

Betty had taken no time at all in getting Rox's poetry to me. I wasn't sure if it was her or Rox who had rushed it, but Aiden handed me the notebook only two days later. I ran my fingertips along the pages, tracing over her doodles in the corners. Most of these poems I had read before, but there were a handful of new ones in the back. My eyes carefully scanned the pages, noticing familiar scenes.

She had written about a raven with broken wings, a rabid pervert squirrel, a fear of going fast, and a fire hose in her pants. I guessed that fire hose was my dick. I giggled my way through her poems, tearing up here and there when she went deep into feelings. She had poured her soul out into those few words and then quickly washed them away with her clever wit.

I wanted to text her to thank her for letting me borrow this book that I knew meant so much to her, but reading through the poems told me she was hurt beyond anything I could do for her. I still needed to wait and let her see for herself that she was deserving of things far greater than I or anyone could give her. Though that wouldn't keep me from trying. My soul still ached to hear her laugh once more.

"Here we go again," Aiden said, eyeing the luggage I clutched in my hand.

I stood in the doorway of Scarlett Herb, prepared for a quick good-bye.

"Only for a short while. I want to visit Mum and Dad. I want to give the homeland a proper good-bye. I'll be back shortly, and hopefully, this time, I really will be ready to settle down and move on in life. I think so anyway." I pulled my brother in for a hug.

"You running off again doesn't bode well for the business. How am I supposed to run this alone now with all the customers you've gotten me?"

"You'll manage. It's not like I'm leaving for two years! I'll be back within a week or two. Promise."

"And DTF? You know they will ask."

"Tell them the truth. Tell them I left to finish healing, and I'll be back when I'm ready. I'm sure they will understand more than anyone. I need closure." I turned to go, heading back toward my awaiting Uber outside.

"Oh, Jay? Can you bring me back some more coffee and Vegemite? Thinking about putting it on the menu. An ode to the homeland. Oi! Oi! Oi!" Aiden called out, stopping me in my tracks.

"Aye! I'll bring you heaps and heaps of it. Oi! Oi! Oi!" I laughed, ducking away and into my ride.

The good thing about flying to Australia from Outer Forks was that I had all the time in the world to read and write. I knew that Rox probably did not want to hear from me now, but I still owed her the poem that had been part of the treaty.

As soon as I hustled to the airport and boarded my plane, I settled into my seat and pulled out the copies I'd made of Rox's poetry. I studied each line, only stopping when I had to board another plane. On my last flight, I finally felt confident enough to deliver my first ever serious poem. Well, halfway serious. I wanted to try her method of humor to soften the blows too. I took a pen and notebook from my laptop case and began the process of bleeding on paper. I didn't stop until I reached Australia.

THIRTEEN

Rox

I slid on my usual black skirt and heels, pulled a fitted gray top over my head, and declared myself ready to go to The Steamy Clam. Of course, I'd been to strip clubs before. But this time would be different. This time, one of our own would be performing her debut—Nikki, aka Crystal Cream Pie. I didn't even know what to expect, but with Nikki, I was prepared to have my mind blown. Whatever it took to get my mind off of Jay.

No matter how busy I had kept myself these last few weeks, I still thought about him often. I would flip through the TV channels and see a nature show based in Australia, I would walk in Target and see a koala nightshirt, or I'd hear a song that he had sung to me to lull me to sleep. I had seen a fire hydrant spewing the other day, and it'd even reminded me of his never-ending dick and the way it popped off like a champagne bottle.

Jay stayed in the back of my mind, no matter what was going on in my life.

I had been so distracted these last few weeks that I wasn't able to focus much on anything. I threw myself into our taco business. Earl purchased us another truck, and training new employees was exhausting. Betty took the lead on that, thankfully, but I still had my hands in a million different things.

My volunteer time at the shelter was cut short as I focused on myself and the healing that I needed to do. I had become one of them—the ladies at the shelter, attending group classes regularly and not just sporadically, as I had done in my past. I fully committed myself to heal my scars and only healing my scars. DTF helped, Earl helped, the shelter helped. But there was still one thing missing that I felt had helped me more than anything. It was him. I missed Jay. His words had made me feel better about myself than I had in years, and I missed that—and him.

On nights I came home late, I always looked out toward his window, but his light was never on anymore. The first time I had seen it was turned off, I'd asked Layla if she'd heard from Aiden how Jay was doing. She'd told me he went back to Australia for business he needed to attend to.

They always run.

"For forever?" I asked Layla.

"No! No! Aiden said just for a little while. He had business to attend to—as in personal business." Layla put her hand on my back and rubbed my shoulders.

"Okay, I guess. I hope he is okay?" I asked, wanting more information than the little bit she had given me.

"I can ask Aiden, but that was all he said. I'm sorry, honey. Are you thinking about trying to start talking to him again? I can see how you haven't been smiling much at all without him. I think he was good for you."

"But I want to be good for him too."

"You are! But I get it. You need to believe that yourself. You're almost there. I think you've put in enough work, and I can tell you're coming around."

"Thanks. I feel better. More confident. I just hope he's still available when I get up enough confidence to step back into a relationship. When he said he loved me, I freaked out a bit. It wasn't so much him saying it out loud, but when he said it, I realized I was falling in love with him too. I got scared. Chickened out. And still, my dumbass mistook his concern for control. I just want to react normally to stuff like that. I still beat myself up over it. I should have just fallen into his arms that night."

Layla put her arms around me. "That would have been dreamy, but it also would have been the wrong thing to do. You did the right thing. Take your time, Rox. Jay will understand, and if he doesn't, then fuck him. There are a million other men out there who would have you in a heartbeat."

"But I'm pretty sure I only want that one heartbeat—his," I whispered into her hair, letting myself collapse into her and cry.

If anyone could understand this gushy side of me, it was Layla.

"I know; I know." She patted my back and stroked my hair, comforting me in her gentle way.

Layla had the motherly instinct that the rest of DTF lacked. We were all supportive and loving, but if we were sick and needed chicken soup, Layla was the one to call. We didn't even need to ask her. She would bring it over along with anything else she could find to cheer us up. When I'd had the flu a few years back, she'd brought me over Chinese takeout, a stack of male porn magazines, a new vibrator, and meds. She stayed up late with me that night, laughing through the magazines and bingeing creepy documentaries on Netflix. As soon as she had left, I'd tested the new vibrator. She was a good friend.

I watched my reflection in the mirror, tracing a dark red color over my lips—the same lipstick I had worn when I first gave Jay a blow job in that sketchy Ferris wheel. I remembered the red ring around his cock as I'd left my mark on him. Now, he was probably in Australia, getting more rings around his cock in whatever color those women over there liked to use. A flare of jealousy flashed through me before I quickly pushed it back down.

I squeezed my small boobs together and tugged down my shirt. Tonight, I was going out to the strip club. And since I had been single and healing, I could afford to have a little fun.

DTF, minus Crystal Cream Pie, sat around the front of the stage. The only person missing from our crew was Earl, but that was because Nikki refused to tell him about tonight. Not that he wouldn't approve. Knowing Earl, he would probably be the one throwing the most money at her. But he was still a father figure to us all, and that was just disgusting. We all agreed to keep Nikki's alter ego under wraps.

I glanced around the packed room, noticing an even number of both men and women. "What's going on tonight besides Crystal's debut? It seems packed!" I asked a topless waitress whose boobs were two seconds from dipping into the cocktails that she had set in front of us. I didn't care for my vodka with a side of nipple, but at the strip club, YOLO.

"We have four debuts tonight—two female, two male. Crystal is our icing on the cake if you ask me, but those boys we got dancing with us tonight, ladies, you just wait. I've never seen anything like it. Sometimes, they put on a skit together and have the woman in the middle, if you know what I mean. Maybe one of you lucky ladies can catch their eye tonight if they do that routine. I'd give anything to be in on that sandwich," she said.

"Dibs!" Layla said.

"Well, there're two. So, we each get one unless Rox here wants a turn. Then, we are going to have to fight it out." Betty took the straw out of her drink and set it on the table before taking a long sip of her cocktail.

"Hmm … let me see what these men look like first," I said, sitting back in my chair as the lights dimmed.

All three of us had our eyes glued to the stage when the first stripper came out. He looked oddly familiar, but I couldn't put my finger on where I had seen him before.

"Terrance! Terrance! Oh my gosh! It's Terrance!" Layla bounced in her seat.

Holy. Fuck, Betty mouthed, leaning forward in her chair.

"Shh! Oh my gosh. I can't believe he works here too! I wonder if Nikki knew this. Why the hell didn't she tell us?" I whispered only loud enough for the girls to hear me.

"I don't know. Don't care. I have been waiting to see what is under that apron of his at the bar. I'm going to enjoy this. Y'all, hush," Betty said.

I had only seen that look in Betty's eyes once before, back when she was dating the race-car driver. That look was dangerous. It meant she was about to devour something, and I was never sure if that was in a good or bad way.

I threw back my drink, not yet sure how I felt about watching Scarlett Herb's bartender, who had been so friendly, about to shake his junk in all of our faces.

"Please welcome Mix Master Tito!" the announcer called from the back.

A single light illuminated Terrance—Tito's—body as he stood in front of a rolling bar cart, waiting for the music to start. True to his other job, he wore an apron, a button-up shirt, and black slacks. I bit my lip, nervous for him.

The music began to play as he looked out into the crowd, caught Betty's eye, and thrust his hips forward. I heard an audible gasp come from her side of the table.

Layla clutched her heart, and Betty's bedroom eyes locked straight back on him.

Ah hell.

Tito ripped off his apron, his button-up, and lastly, his slacks, revealing nothing but a skimpy banana hammock. I didn't have a clue how fast he had done all of that. I thought to myself that maybe he had a third job as a quick-change artist at a sideshow.

"Oh my gosh! Look at those muscles!" Layla squealed.

Tito spun around, splashing some liquor into a cocktail shaker, turning around again and shaking it so hard that his dick flopped around like a snake rearing back, ready to strike. I watched Betty's head bob up and down in rhythm as he shook himself over to her. He humped the air down to the floor and slid on his back, stopping right in front of us. His hips rose, pumping his johnson up and down hard before he slowly poured whatever concoction he'd made in his shaker right over his abs.

He set the shaker down, got to his knees, and gyrated in front of us. The alcohol ran down his rippled chest, and he curled his finger and motioned for Betty to come here. She only had to move a few feet, and she would be in line with his whole package, which she took no time in doing. I shook my head as I watched Tito point to his abs and nod. Betty smiled, stuck her tongue out, and ran it from his navel to a nipple.

The crowd went wild. Mostly women, but some of the men even cheered for Betty. I couldn't contain my laughter as I watched them flirt onstage. He pulled her up there, pushing her against the pole as he danced around her. Betty being Betty danced right back at him. They dry-humped each other until the song ended, and then he kissed her hand and helped her back offstage.

Layla and I both stared at Betty, waiting on her to say something.

"What?" Betty plopped herself back into her chair, pursed her lips, and finished her drink.

"What do you mean, *what*? That was the hottest striptease I'd ever seen! And to think, he is such a sweet bartender. I had no idea he was a ferocious beast," Layla growled.

"Your ferocious beast owns Scarlett Herb, trick, so sit down. That one *I'll* be taking home." Betty snapped her fingers in the air and ended the conversation.

"Aiden is just a friend! Y'all need to stop it with all of that!" Layla crossed her arms and sat back.

"Shh! It's her turn!" I shushed my two horny friends and focused on the next act.

Two nearly naked ladies cleaned up the wet stage before Crystal Cream Pie made her entrance.

"Fuck, this is amazing." I laughed.

Betty and Layla nodded in agreement as we fell into the Cream Pie trance.

Nikki—Crystal—sauntered to the center of the stage in a sexy waitress outfit. She, too, had a rolling cart behind her, complete with cream pies. As the music began to play, she swung herself around the pole, climbing upside down and dropping to the floor in one quick movement that made all three of our jaws fall open.

We watched, wide-eyed, while she stripped her tiny shirt off and threw it into the crowd. A tall, bearded man caught it, sniffed it, and stuffed it in his pocket while he licked his lips and eye-fucked her.

"Well, that escalated quickly." Betty's eyebrows shot up into her hairline.

"Not like you were any less freak nasty up there onstage," I muttered back to her.

Nikki tore her bra off, exposing her perky knockers to us all. The men hollered out, but we just nodded. It wasn't like we hadn't seen them before. She was known for whipping them out whenever. With Nikki, she didn't stick her butt out to moon people as a joke. She raised her top and shook her boobs, just like she was doing now. She turned her back toward us and bent over, twerking her butt cheeks from side to side. I let out a loud whistle among the fifty others cheering her on. A group of men had gathered closer to the stage, throwing money out in front of her. She turned to us and winked before grabbing two of the cream pies off of the cart.

"What do you think she's going to—oh my gosh!" Layla gasped as Crystal Cream Pie smashed the pies right onto her titties.

She gyrated back down to the crowd of men, sticking one of their heads right between her breasts, so he could give her a whipped-cream motorboat. She shook her boobs in his face and then his friend's face, and Layla even rushed to the stage to get boobs in her face too.

"What the hell, girl? What's wrong with you?" Betty's voice trailed off as she shook her head at Layla.

"I wanted to get in on the fun too! Plus, I slipped a twenty in her G-string. Women supporting women," she answered, picking up a napkin and wiping the whipped cream off of her cheeks.

"DTF!" I raised my glass to Nikki as she finished up her dance and disappeared backstage.

Everyone, including us, gave her a standing ovation.

"What a badass," Betty said as we all laughed.

I felt like I needed to take a cold shower already.

"That was amazing. This is amazing. Thanks for taking me out tonight, girls. Glad we could come together and support one of our own." I smiled.

"Just like we have been supporting you, love. I know it's been tough these last few weeks, but we are still here for ya." Layla reached across to squeeze my hand.

"It's good you're getting out. I know you're finally coming around and being your old self again. I can see it in your eyes. You're almost there. You've got this, Rox," Betty said, winking at me.

"Thanks, ladies. One day at a time. This certainly helped. I've got some new inspiration at least. I think I'll write a poem about cream pies. I need to make it funnier though. Maybe I'll have her sit in it instead of rubbing it on her chest." I shrugged.

"Lawd, don't give that child any more ideas." Betty shook her head.

I hadn't had a night packed with this much fun since I could remember. I looked at every one of my friends, the sexy strippers slinging around their schlongs, and the money flying through the air. I thought to myself how it only seemed like yesterday that I had been in a very dark place. And now, I was beginning to see a lighter place. Even if that light was only the flickering neon lights of a strip club, it was still better than where I had been.

We stayed at The Steamy Clam until it shut down, laughing, talking, drinking, and catcalling men, women, and each other. Terrance even appeared again to give Betty an encore. Nikki explained all about stripper code and how she couldn't tell us about him but wanted Betty to be shocked when she found out her favorite flirty bartender could bust a move anyway. We left the club exhilarated.

When my Uber dropped me off back at my house, I instinctively looked toward Jay's window in hopes that his light would be turned on. It wasn't. I felt a slight lingering sadness, but I put one foot in front of the other, tilted my chin up, and marched through my door.

It had been two weeks since Crystal Cream Pie's debut when the girls said that they wanted to take me out for another fun night. They had said we would go to The Lounge later this evening since it was poetry night, but I needed to dress up because we were going out afterward. Betty mentioned drinks at Scarlett Herb, so I needed to wear something classy and sexy. I wasn't sure that I was ready yet to make as big of a step as going to Scarlett Herb again, but she insisted it would help me with any closure I might need.

It had been nearly two months since I last saw or heard from Jay. Aiden stopped by his place every so often to check on things. I only knew that because he had bumped into me outside one of the times. It had been slightly awkward, but he'd made sure to tell me that Jay was coming back and that he was only finishing up some business.

I thought about the night of our argument often and how it was a big misunderstanding on both of our parts. We were both broken. He was, too, whether he could admit it or not.

I smoothed down my dress and settled into Betty's car. She had volunteered to pick us all up tonight and be the designated driver. That was extremely out of character for her, so I was already on edge when we arrived at poetry night.

"Wow! Look at you!" Betty said.

The rest of DTF whistled from the backseat.

"Thanks! You all look pretty hot yourselves!" I said, nodding at my girls.

We chatted about our day but mostly drove in silence, which, again, was unusual. I didn't know if it was the nervousness of heading to Scarlett Herb looming over my head or what.

"What is this?" I asked as soon as we pulled up to The Lounge.

I had never seen so many cars here before. There wasn't an empty parking space available around the entire building. Betty circled the lot several times, ultimately deciding on parking across the street.

"No clue," DTF answered in unison.

I glanced at Layla and Nikki in the backseat. Layla had a smile on her that stretched from ear to ear, and Nikki avoided my eyes. Something was up. A feeling of unease settled in my stomach.

"Bullshit. Is something going on with the shelter tonight? Betty! Look at me. I know you won't lie to me. What is it?" I asked, panic rising in my voice.

"Oh, Rox. I wish I could say. Let's just go check it out, okay?" Betty's eyes looked around everywhere but at me.

I scooted down into my seat, wondering what trouble I was about to walk into. I closed my eyes, concentrating on any significant events that I had forgotten about. A mental calendar of everyone's birthdays ran through my head until it landed on Earl's upcoming sixtieth celebration.

"Is this Earl's birthday party? Why wouldn't you tell me?" I sat back up, turning in my seat to give death stares at the girls in the back.

"It's not Earl's birthday," Nikki mumbled, tugging at the crystal that hung around her neck. Her eyes shifted toward Layla, who was shaking her knee back and forth.

Betty pulled into an empty spot across the street.

I hopped out of the car as fast as I could. The awkward silence that hung in the air felt suffocating. "Whatever. I'll go see for myself."

"Rox, wait. Wait for us," Betty said. She had that tone in her voice that only came out when she meant business.

I'd heard it plenty of times before, and I trusted my best friend. I knew well enough to listen to her when her voice became sharp-edged.

I swallowed hard and took a deep breath, hoping I wasn't walking into a funeral. DTF's usual silly mood was much less fun and much more serious.

Why the fuck isn't anyone telling me what's going on?

"Come on." Layla put her arm around me and offered up a quick smile before dragging me into The Lounge.

We opened the doors to the crowded bar.

"Congratulations!" came voice after voice around me as I elbowed my way through the crowd.

I looked back to Betty, who followed me closely behind, and shook my head.

What did I do? I mouthed back to her.

I noticed friends from the shelter and regular customers from the truck, and I thought I'd even spotted my old uncle Mark. Everyone wore a smile, gave me a thumbs-up, told me congratulations, or clapped me on the back.

"Is this because we expanded The Pink Taco Truck?"

"No! It's not the tacos. It's you. You fixed your broken wings, Rox. And everyone else's." Betty pushed me forward, steering me with her hands on my shoulders.

I guessed she was pushing me to our usual corner table.

"I'm not fixed yet! I don't understand," I said above the cheering of the crowd. "How?" The words caught in my throat as I noticed Jay sitting at the corner table.

Betty let go of my shoulders and disappeared. Jay stood up as soon as he saw me, coming to my aid because, somehow, he knew I was about to fall.

"Rox," Jay said, rushing to my side and taking me in his arms.

My heartbeat slowed the second I felt his touch. All of the confusion and chaos melted away, leaving just me and him standing there. He felt like home.

"What's going on, Jay? I thought you were back in Australia?" I peeled myself off of him, so I could search his eyes.

"I did go back home—unfinished business. I visited my parents' graves and told them the good-bye I never got to tell them. I grieved—for weeks. I quit running, and I just let myself feel and be human. I holed myself up in a hotel and walked through hell. I'm not going to lie, Rox; I'm still going through hell. But at least now, I'm crawling out of it. It's slowly disappearing behind me. I realized I didn't need to run to forget. I only needed to stay put. My marathon wasn't running away. It was dragging myself *through* the worst experiences of my life, slowly putting one foot in front of the other. I was in a bad, bad place. But I have you to thank for setting me on the path to getting out of it."

I put my hand to my chest as if to keep my heart from breaking out of my rib cage. My pulse thumped through my veins hard, causing me to wince.

"I didn't do anything. That healing, that was all you. You did the hard stuff, and you still are. You always will be. Thank you for being open. I was very sad when you left. I thought when the girls told me you had unfinished business, you were working back in Australia. I didn't know you were healing. I had nothing to do with that."

"No. I would never leave you if you hadn't told me to. I knew you needed space, and that was just another hard thing I had to do. I know you had to heal too. But really, you had everything to do with my healing. This is my way of saying thanks."

He took my hand and led me to the back corner table, where stacks of books lay piled high.

"What is this?" I picked up a book and ran my fingertips over the gold-flecked cover. I brought it closer to my eyes as I squinted in the dark to try to read the title.

Kintsugi
By Roxanne Corvus

I set it down and grabbed the sides of the table, steadying myself.

"Is this what I think it is? My poems? How did they …" I picked the book back up, thumbing through the pages and reading my poems. I flipped to the front.

You don't have to laugh to keep from crying. You are capable of doing both, read the inscription.

I gasped, covering my mouth with my hand.

"Did you do this?" I whispered, falling onto a chair.

"Depends. If you're mad about it, I'm going to blame Betty. If not, it was all me. You did tell me you wanted to publish them one day." Jay sat down beside me, scooting his chair closer so that our knees touched.

He dipped his head to catch my eyes, but I didn't look up. I couldn't even lift my gaze.

"Rox? You okay?" he said, reaching out to rub my knee.

I opened my mouth to speak, but instead, I let myself cry. He pulled me over into his lap and pressed my body tight against his. I let myself feel the pain, the shock, and the joy that flooded my emotions. It wasn't until half an hour later that I realized where I was and noticed my poems were being read in the background by DTF.

I wiped my eyes with a scratchy napkin and squeezed Jay's hand as we both turned our attention to the small stage and listened. Betty read about escaping nightmares and ferocious taco-eating dinosaurs. Layla read about finding self-worth and a rabid, perverted squirrel. I laughed and cried through the reenactments that she gestured with her hands and hips.

"Still was a hot fuck in the woods. Squirrel or not," Jay whispered in my ear, sitting up.

"The best." I nodded.

"Mmhmm," he growled back at me, his hands tight on my hips.

I melted into his lap, feeling him harden underneath me.

" 'Divine Intervention,' " Nikki read, clearing her throat loudly and turning her attention toward Jay and me in the back.

"I didn't write that," I whispered, shifting around on his lap.

His dick felt like a steel rod jabbing me from behind.

"I did," he said, nervously bouncing his knees, which sent me bouncing too.

My body shook back and forth as I held on to the arms of the chair.

"What are we doing? Playing Ride the Horsey? I can't listen if you're bucking me to the ground."

"Sorry. Sorry." He stilled his legs.

"Are you two ready or what?" Nikki said into the microphone.

We turned our attention back toward her and the crowd that had been watching our entire antics, laughing.

"Right! Let's hear it. Sorry about that!" Jay called loudly, nodding for Nikki to begin.

"Ahem," Nikki said, clearing her throat.

"Divine Intervention"
I think of you,
And the battles of my past
Melt away,
As if your fingertips are flames,
Bringing me out of this ice
I've been frozen inside of for
Far too long.
You flew into my life,
Your wings unfurled.
Majestic Raven,
Wrapped in gold
Crystal spells
Witch's brew.
Stars aligned,
And I found you.
I roamed the earth,
And I found you.
I knew you.
I've always known you.
In another lifetime,
You were mine,
And I was yours.
And now, we are here,
Together.
I am home.

When Nikki finished, I let out my breath that I'd held during the entire poem.

"You really feel that way?" I asked, taking deep breaths to steady myself.

"Absolutely." Jay brushed my hair out of my face.

"Do you know that before you came into my life, I had never had a man show me even a fraction of the kindness that you have? That the first time we came here, you pulled my chair out for me, and I was confused because I didn't know what you were doing that for or what it meant. I thought maybe you were looking for me to repay you in sex or something when you did these nice things. I've never had someone be so patient, kind, and loving with me."

"Fuck those fuckers and their fucking bullshit. You deserve patience, kindness, love, and all the good things in life," he growled, circling his arms around me even tighter.

"So do you. I want to apologize for pushing you away. I'm really sorry I just wasn't ready to understand how to be normal in a normal and healthy relationship. I'm still slowly learning myself again. Just so you know, I am a work in progress. But I also want you to know that I've known my true feelings for you for a while now. Even if I fought against them because they scared me. I knew from that moment you ordered me an On the Rox cocktail and licked my pussy underneath the prim-and-proper tablecloth of your restaurant. I knew then that I loved you, Jay Taylor. Squirrel phobia and all. I didn't just appear for you at the right time, but you appeared for me at the right time too."

"I know. I guess it was just meant to be."

"Some of that divine intervention." I smiled, reaching into my bra and pulling out the rose quartz stone Nikki had given me months ago.

"Ha! The universe is speaking to us," he said, shifting to put his hand in his pocket and pulling out a similar rose quartz crystal.

"So, that really was a rock in your pocket! Thought so! Damn near felt like steel!" I laughed.

"For you. All for you, Kintsugi." He pressed his lips to mine and made out with me in the corner to the sounds of my poems from my badass book being read in the background.

"You two need to get a damn room," Betty said, rudely interrupting my dry-hump session.

"Let them enjoy it. While they're still young," Earl muttered behind her.

Layla, Nikki, Aiden, and even Terrance gathered around our table.

"Did you tell her the best part?" Layla looked back and forth from Jay to me.

"I haven't had the honor yet. How about you tell her?" Jay winked at Layla, who clearly couldn't hold back her excitement any longer.

"Ten percent of proceeds on the book is set up to go straight to the shelter!" she blurted out.

"What? Really? Oh my gosh! You thought of everything! Wow!" I hugged Jay. My smile grew so wide that my cheeks ached.

"You did well. Proud of you. Both of you. Guess that means I'm not getting that Crocodile Dundee handbag." Betty pursed her lips and raised her brows at Jay.

"Guess not. But if you prefer a furry squirrel bag, I might be able to help you out there," he replied, making even Betty break her fierce gaze and laugh.

"Looks like you'd better get to signing!" Nikki handed me a pen and motioned toward the line that had begun to form in front of us.

"Right!" I hopped off of Jay's lap and smoothed down my skirt. "Let's do it!"

"Quick toast! Quick toast!" Aiden called as a waitress brought over several glasses of champagne.

"To Rox! To Jay! To new beginnings!" Layla shouted, bouncing on her heels.

"And to DTF!" I added.

"DTF!" my best friends shouted back.

We clinked our glasses together before I settled into a chair and picked up a book to begin signing. Jay sat down beside me, scooting in close.

"Look at my wild raven, flying free." He smiled. His eyes glistened as he blinked back tears.

"Ravens mate for life, ya know. So, I guess you could say they have soul mates. Want to soar through the sky with me?" I asked as I began to sign my first book.

"Let's go fast." He leaned into me, kissing my cheek.

EPILOGUE

Jay

"**W**here does this box go?" I asked Rox. My back ached from carrying her moving boxes for two days. So far, we had cleared her home out of everything, except her master bedroom. She had kept that door shut since I had known her.

"You can set it in the kitchen." Rox sat on the floor of my living room, unboxing books, candles, and whatever else she'd brought over from her witch's lair.

"Well, this is the last one. Everything else is gone, cleared out. What about your master bedroom? What are you going to do with it all? Betty isn't going to want your old furniture in her new house." I set the box down in the kitchen, jumping over the obstacle course of knickknacks strung out in our living room.

"Burn it," Rox said without looking up.

"Rox! You can't burn it! Aiden and I can take care of it if you don't want to set foot in there. I understand."

"DTF will help too. I'm sorry, Jay. I just can't go back into that room ever again. I don't want to see any of that stuff from my old life. I'm ridding myself of all of it. This is a fresh start for me." She lifted herself off the floor and put her arms around me.

"It's a fresh start for me too. And do you know what I like to do with something new?" I asked, sweeping her off her feet and cradling her in my arms.

"What's that?" She smiled, pulling herself up to meet my lips.

"Fuck in every room. We have to christen it," I muttered into her mouth.

"Oh, is that what you were doing that day when I saw you spew your load on the couch? You were christening it?" she said, pulling back from me and laughing.

"Damn! I told you that you'd never let that go."

"I'm sorry! You just left the door open for that one. I had to take it. Let's christen every single room, starting with … this one. It's not like your couch hasn't seen jizz before!"

"And … you're still going." I carried her to the couch and sat her down, wincing as she brushed against my forearm.

She stuck her hand out and gently ran her fingertips over my wrapped tattoo.

"It's still sore?" she asked, pouting her lips.

"Just a little. Nothing I can't handle though. I'm tough as nails." I rubbed my hand across the drawing of my homeland.

The tattoo artist had filled in my country with our flag and my mum's and dad's initials. I had decided against my poor cat's face and marked myself with my story. I smiled, finally on the other side of grief and looking forward to the next chapter of my life.

"No, you're tough as a railroad spike, Jay Taylor. Now, get over here and fuck me in my—*our* new lair!" She cackled.

"Lair? Can't we call it a nest?" I groaned, looking down at her perfect body.

My cock stirred, lengthening down my leg. Her eyes widened at the bulge in my pants.

"We are going to have to hash this one out. But for now, come get on the Rox!" She pulled her top up over her head, flinging it across the room.

"On the Rox!" I smiled. "That's the best damn way to take life. With you by my side. Or under me." I grinned, hopping on top of her and smothering her with my love.

THE END

WANT MORE DTF?
READ ON FOR THE FIRST CHAPTER
FROM *CREAM-PIED.*

CREAM-PIED ONE

Nikki

Crowds gathered at The Steamy Clam every Saturday night since I'd made my debut onstage and twirled around the pole. I had made eight hundred dollars that night, and by the size of the audience tonight, I hoped I could make even more. I wasn't entirely broke, but a string of bad boyfriends had left me in a mountain of debt that I'd been digging my way out of for years. For some reason, I attracted the laziest, trashiest, and brokest douche bags around.

With my time pulled between working two jobs, I barely made it to my new passion, volunteering with disadvantaged youth at the cottage. Those kids had seen and lived some of the darkest moments imaginable. I wasn't a stranger to that life either, so I did my best to help them through that. We would work on art projects, play sports, and do homework or anything else that came up. The most important gift I could give the children was my steady and positive presence in their lives. That was why I had been running myself crazy, working at The Steamy Clam at night. I planned on quitting after I paid off my debt and devoted more time to do the volunteer work that made me truly happy and fulfilled.

Of course, my life as a dancer had been kept under wraps at the cottage. Not because I was ashamed of my job, but because most people found that depressing as hell. The stigma surrounding strip clubs always included blow and prostitution. But in my experience, it was all about women supporting other women and a judgment-free zone. Still, I couldn't go around, telling children that. The kids at the cottage all knew me as the taco truck lady who had risen above her traumatic childhood and was making it on her own. Of course, I had also left out the fact that I was broker than shit because of my dumbass ex-boyfriends.

At this point in my life, I was finally getting my shit together. I felt a calling to let the youth of the world know that they could rise above the shitty cards they'd been dealt too.

I swiped a bold lipstick across my lips and readied myself in front of the mirror, carefully sticking red heart pasties over my nipples and adjusting my G-string. I shook my fingers through my hair, fluffing it up and out until it looked like I'd stuck my finger in an electric socket. Bigger was always better—with everything.

The last dancer, Kiki, filed in, pulling money from her boots and G-string and winking at me. Kiki had taught me the ropes of the club not long ago. She had been working the pole for six years and helped me nail all of my spins, climbs, and inverted moves.

"Those are the moneymaking tricks," she had told me back when I was fresh meat at the club.

Men loved it when dancers were facedown and ass up, gyrating on the pole. If I could hold myself upside down while booty-popping for twenty seconds, she had told me that I would earn double my usual payout per dance. I'd made a mental note to work on staying up as long as possible and slowing the blood rush to my head. The quicker I was paid, the faster I was gone out of here.

Of course, no one back home in the trailer park I had grown up in would be surprised that foul-mouthed Nikki Vinco had grown up to become Crystal Cream Pie, Outer Fork's most eligible stripper. At least, I didn't have the ten kids and ten different baby daddies that everyone had expected in my future.

I knocked on wood and counted down the days until my period as I left the dressing room and headed toward the stage. Babies wouldn't ever be in my future. I still wasn't even sure if I wanted a husband. My friends with benefits had worked well for me over the last few years, and now that I was twenty-eight, I still didn't feel my biological clock ticking.

I preferred working with older kids. The kids old enough to wipe their butts and blow their noses. I wasn't at a point in my life where anything remotely like having a family was in my future. I had wanted the whole sit-down-around-the-dinner-table family dynamic when I was younger, but after living without it for so long, I had been disillusioned not to care. It was probably all fake anyway. I had seen more than enough wedding rings on the hands of men slipping dollar bills into my panties.

I had no shame, working as Crystal Cream Pie. If I had to get my hands dirty to get where I was supposed to be in life, I would. Besides, stripping was only my side hustle. My full-time job was on board The Pink Taco Truck with my DTF crew. Dirty. Tough. Female. I couldn't think of a better way to describe our girl gang.

My friends had supported me throughout my string of bad men, and I'd done the same for them. We all had stories to tell and drama to air, but luckily, this year, things were beginning to fall into place for all of us. With steady money from the taco truck and my side gig of dancing, my debt grew smaller and smaller, which meant financial independence was quickly becoming within reach—finally.

I sauntered out onto the stage and looked out into the crowd. My palm gripped around the pole, and I let myself fall into it and twirl before wrapping my legs around it and climbing up. The music echoed off the walls, drowning out the men catcalling me from the side of the stage. I winked at them all, blew kisses, and performed a few tricks in the air before crashing down into the splits. I humped my way across the floor in a move called The Snail Trail and made my way toward the guests shaking their money at me. I shoved my boobs in everyone's faces and motorboated my way to a debt-free life.

This is so easy.

I pushed myself up to my knees and crawled back to the pole. My gig was almost up, and I needed to flip upside down, so these horny men would lose their control and throw all their money at me. I wrapped my legs around the cold steel and climbed to the top, looking out and into the crowd. A tall man with a lumberjack beard sat, watching me from a dark corner in the back. I had noticed him plenty of times over the last few weeks, but he hadn't yet made his way close enough to the stage to stuff any money in my bra. He stayed in that corner night after night but never once asked me for a lap dance.

I sat at the top of the pole, leaning back onto my hand and spreading my legs as wide as they could go before readying myself to flip over. I stared at the bearded man in the back, locking eyes with him. He reached up to stroke his beard and stared back, eye-fucking me from across the room. I began to slip as my palms and the rest of my body broke out into a sweat. I held on as tight as I could, but it was no use. I couldn't make my inverted moves. I couldn't even hang on. When the song came to a stop, so did I— crashing down and landing so hard on my half-naked ass that the sound of my downfall echoed across the suddenly silent room.

The tall, bearded man stood up, leering at me as if he had an internal conflict on making his next move. His hand clutched his heart underneath a flannel shirt.

Kiki rushed to my side, helping me hobble offstage.

"Are you okay? You didn't hurt anything other than your ego, right?" Layla said after I told her and the rest of DTF about my fall at The Steamy Clam.

"She didn't even hurt that. Don't you know Nikki by now? She doesn't give any fucks. She picked herself up and moved on," Betty said, shaking her head at Layla.

"Well, I would have been mortified! I wouldn't be able to show my face, or my ass, again at that club. Do you think it will hurt your Crystal Cream Pie career?" Layla asked.

"First of all, it's not my career. And most of those men were so drunk, they probably forgot about it before the night ended anyway." I shrugged, hopping out of the taco truck to set up tables.

A line already snaked out into the street, and we weren't set to open for another fifteen minutes.

"You sure you're okay?" Rox said, following behind me.

"Yep. I'll manage. It wasn't that big of a deal," I sighed.

"No. Come here. Look at me." Rox reached out and grabbed my arm.

"Fine. My ego was hurt a little. But just a little. And only because of this guy there." I slumped my shoulders forward.

Typically, men were easy for me to figure out, but my hairy stalker distracted me.

"What man?" Rox asked.

"This lumberjack guy. He is there every night, watching me. I can't figure out if it's creepy or flattering. Anyway, I think his stare made me lose my grip and crash. I don't know. Can't figure it out. He's not my type anyway. I've never really cared for beards, and he was dressed in flannel."

"Beards and flannel, eh? Maybe he was about to go to a hoedown."

"Exactly. Not my type. No business suits, no making it rain on me, no spoiling me like how I deserve. You know I had a man pay me six hundred dollars for a thirty-minute lap dance the other day? That's what I'm looking for—but on a regular basis. Someone who has enough money never to get me in debt."

"And you damn well deserve it. You're worth that and more. Don't settle for another broke loser," Rox said before returning to our task.

I watched her set the tables up as she smiled and hummed, dancing around the parking lot. The hot summer sun shone down on her in a way that lit her up like an angel. Though I knew none of us were angels, Rox would be the closest to anything spiritually positive. She was my hero. This time last year, none of us had been humming, smiling, or laughing. But today, Rox's fresh attitude brought me back to my truth and the task before me of moving up and moving on.

I clasped my palm around the iolite crystal that hung around my neck. When I had read that iolite increased financial well-being, I'd placed the crystal everywhere in my home. I always kept it around my neck as a reminder that I alone could take control of my situation and improve my life—even if that meant rolling around half-naked on a stage.

"Come get your grub on!" Betty shouted out the window, ringing the dinner bell that Layla had recently installed on the truck.

"Shit! I'm not ready yet!" I yelled. I threw the tables and chairs together as quickly as possible, aware of the customers rolling their eyes and tapping their feet around me.

We were parked at the corporate park again today, which meant our customers were typically impatient buttholes—Bluetooth in the ear, no manners, no tips.

DTF had asked me not long ago if I wanted to take charge of our new taco truck that frequented the other side of town, but I politely declined. I didn't want to lose my friends. If I couldn't come to work every day, laughing and being my inappropriate self, then I didn't want to even go into work. Lately, my life had been heading slowly in the direction I was hoping for. I didn't want to jinx myself. Besides, Mercury had been in retrograde when they asked me. That had been a big hell no from me.

"Come on," Rox said, pulling my arm back to the kitchen. "Jay is stopping by for lunch, and I need to work through this crowd, so I can catch a quick break when he gets here." A mischievous grin played across her lips.

"I swear you haven't stopped smiling since divine intervention led you two together. I need that to happen to me. Think a rich, hot sex god will fall out of the sky and save me from making the same mistakes I did with the broke douche bags of my past?" I asked, climbing into the truck.

"Nope. And if he did, you are still going to work your ass off to be an independent woman and not ever depend on a damn man," Betty said, handing me an apron.

"I hate to admit it, but Betty is right. I still have faith you'll find your Prince Charming!" Layla gushed. Her eyes darted off dreamily into the distance.

"Not sure I want a Prince Charming, but I'll take a Lord of the Underworld. We can dress in leather, tie each other up with chains, and perform tantric sex under the full moon. Maybe throw some whiskey shots in there, and that would be my ideal night," I said, nodding my head in agreement with the love life I had planned for my future.

"Good Lord!" Betty shook her head.

"Well, sex under a full moon sounds romantic at least," Layla sighed.

When I returned to The Steamy Clam on Saturday night, after I had literally busted a move during my last performance, I noticed the same bearded man at the same corner table, staring at me with the same intense gaze. I couldn't shake his stare off of me the entire night. When my time to shine came up, I purposely avoided eye contact with him so that, hopefully, I wouldn't slip and fall flat on my face. I tried to check in with my inner soul and figure out what the hell emotions she was feeling, but my inner soul had no answers either.

I finished my routine and headed toward the back to clean the cream off my boobs. I cream-pied my tits at least once every night because, well, that was what the men— and some women—loved. Everyone loved to stick their face in a chest full of whipped cream—everyone but Beard Man. Not once had he come up to the stage. He only enjoyed a free show from the back.

I huffily brushed a towel over myself, cleaning off the sticky residue from my chest—cream, slobber, and I didn't even want to know what else.

"Nikki! Someone wants a lap dance in the private room." Kiki came running backstage, unbuckling her bra and throwing it to the side. She slipped the rest of her clothes off and began to squirm her way into a schoolgirl costume.

"Who is it? A regular?" I asked, hoping it was the man who'd paid me the big bucks not long ago.

I reached for the whip, remembering he liked it when I spanked him. He was married. He deserved to be whipped. He was an easy client.

"No, I don't know this one," she called before scurrying off again.

I checked my reflection in the mirror, making sure I didn't have any hidden cream in my drawers, and made my way back out into the club and toward the back room. Our private room was the sleaziest room imaginable. We even had one of those leg lamps sitting on a corner table next to a leather couch. It had to be leather because whatever was left in this room after a private show would need to be wiped off. Not that I ever went that far with my clients, but some men were known to explode on touch.

Kiki had told me, one time, she'd backed her ass up into a man and bounced so hard that he jizzed all over his pants and her. He left a wet spot on the leather that she had to clean up. She hadn't been happy about that, but at least the man had shamefully tipped her more money than she ever made in one night.

I opened the door to the private room, readying myself to bounce my ass clear up to the ceiling. I had only a few hundred dollars left to pay off on one of my credit cards before I could cut it up and throw it out.

I slipped inside the room and shut the door behind me.

"Marry me," came a gruff voice from the dark.

When my eyes adjusted to the darkness in the room, I saw my bearded stalker, down on one knee and presenting me with a wedding ring—a ridiculously large diamond wedding ring. I held my breath while my mind raced as to how best to approach this creepy situation.

"You can't marry someone you don't know! Get up! What's wrong with you?" I spazzed out, straightening myself up to my full height of six feet. I was hoping, if this man was about to pull out a knife, he would get the point that I could be just as crazy, if not crazier.

The man's lips turned down as he shut the jewelry box and pulled himself to his feet, towering over me. The tip of his beard reached the tip of my head. He stood still, looking down at me without saying a word.

"Hey! Earth to the Green Giant up there!" I yanked his beard.

The man's jaw dropped, and his eyes grew wide as he gasped. "You can't treat Dan like that!" He clutched his chest.

"Well, Dan, who refers to himself in the third person, I can't marry you. Sorry! Now, did you want a dance or what?" I put my hands to my hips and my foot in the air, ready to kick him over and onto the couch so I could get this show on the road.

"You're not marrying Dan. You're marrying me." His brows furrowed as if I had offended him.

"No, I'm not marrying you, Dan!" I huffed. This was getting ridiculous.

"I know you're not! It's me! Weston!" he cried, shaking his head.

"I don't know a Weston! Where is Weston, Dan? Who is me?"

At this point, even I was confused. I looked around the room but didn't notice a Weston or Dan or whoever hiding in a corner.

"I'm Weston!" Weston groaned, shoving the jewelry box in his pocket and taking a seat on the sticky leather couch.

"I thought you were Dan!" I crossed my arms over my chest and stuck my fists in my pits so that I wouldn't punch him in his face. The clock was ticking, and I wasn't getting paid to stand here and argue with his split personality.

"This is Dan!" he said, pointing to his beard.

I blinked. "Your beard?"

"Yes!" He threw his hands in the air.

"Your beard is named Dan?"

"Finally! Bingo! You got it!"

"Are you fucking kidding me?"

"No. Now, will you marry me—Weston!" His voice rose in an octave I'd never heard before on a grown man. Maybe a gremlin, but not a grown man.

"No! I will not marry you, Weston. I also won't marry Dan!" I reached out and flicked his beard, making him gasp again.

"This is just not working. I thought you were the one. I was wrong, I guess." He slumped his shoulders forward and put his head in his hands.

I took a deep breath, realizing I could be dealing with someone a few crayons short of a full box. Empathy kicked in.

Thanks, inner soul. Where the fuck have you been?

"Look, you can't propose to someone you don't know. What if we were married and stuck together for the rest of our lives, and I liked the thermostat set at seventy, and you liked it set at eighty-four?"

"That's too hot! I would never!" Weston muttered into his hands.

"Ugh! Point being, I can't commit to someone I don't know, and neither should you! No matter if she is a hot piece of ass who can shake her moneymaker."

"Wait a minute. You want me to commit to you?" He laughed, leaning back onto the couch and spreading his arms to rest against the back cushions.

"Oh my gosh, Weston—Dan—whoever you are, you just asked me to marry you! That's a commitment! Are you on drugs or something? This is insane. I've got to go. I have other clients who would be paying me right now, and that's what I need—money. Not a man groveling at my feet who doesn't even know his real name."

"I'm Weston Banks." He cleared his throat. "I didn't want you to come in here and dance for me. I don't need that. I also didn't want you to *marry me*, marry me."

I sucked in my breath. I had heard that name before. His family owned Westy's amusement park, the diner, a hotel, and pretty much everything else on that side of town. I bit my lip, second-guessing my decision to marry someone who had more money than I'd likely ever see in my lifetime. I glanced at his flannel shirt and scuffed boots. He certainly didn't look the part of wealthy old money.

"That's what marrying means. It's a commitment. You were on one knee. What do you mean, *marry you*, marry you?"

"It's fake. The ring! And the wedding. Or there will be no wedding. I just need you to be my fake fiancée. Only for a little while—until my parents sign over their properties to me instead of my shithole brother, Wes. They are about to retire, and it's been an ongoing feud for over a year. They want to make sure I am carrying on the Banks tradition, and that starts with getting married and having babies."

I pinched the bridge of my nose and plopped myself on the couch next to him. "I know who you are. I thought you took control of the park and hotel and all already."

"No. I wish. Those are rumors. I'm trying to though. I think I can do a better job at it, but don't tell my mama that!"

I sank into the couch.

"Let me get this straight, Weston. You want me to pretend to be your fiancée for a while, so your parents sign over their assets to you instead of your asshat brother, Wes? Which, by the way, what the fuck? Your names are so damn confusing. Anyway, moving on. What do I get out of pretending? You said that ring is fake. So, what's in this for me? Why would I want to put up with the stress and Dan?"

"Because, first of all, Dan's fucking awesome." He stroked his beard. "And secondly, you said you wanted money. I have plenty. That's never been a concern of mine. Rather I didn't have it, to be honest. I don't need it."

Good. I do.

"How long do I have to play this charade? And what all does it entail?" I sighed.

"Not long at all. You'll accompany me to my family's big Fourth of July celebration. We make up a good story and set a wedding date—a fake one, relax. And then, boom, you are free once I sign. I'll say you left me."

"What? Why do I have to be the bad guy? Maybe you're a cheating bastard!"

"I would never! We can come up with something. Do you think that would work? Are you willing to get into some harmless shenanigans with me?"

My eyes trailed over his pouty lips tucked inside his bushed-out beard. His eyes could only be described as harmless.

"If you pay me well enough and don't be an asshole, then it's a deal."

I stuck my hand out to shake his hand. His long, bony fingers gently wrapped around my palm. I absentmindedly bit my lip and lowered my eyes to do a bulge check. If his dick size was in tune with his height, maybe I could make another friend with benefits—in the plural, meaning sex and spoiling, even if he was awkward as fuck.

"Deal," he said.

"Why didn't you just lead with the fact that you only wanted me to be your fake fiancée instead of freaking me out like that?" I asked.

"Because you're a hot piece of ass who can shake her moneymaker, and I thought it would be worth a try to have you as mine if you let me." He shrugged.

"Nice try, Dan." I gently ran my palm down his beard before bopping his nose with my fingertip. I pushed myself off the couch and headed toward the door.

"Can I at least still get a lap dance?" he said, reaching out and grabbing my arm before I could get away.

"Really? Ugh! I have a feeling this fake marriage is going to last all of two days. Tomorrow night, Scarlett

Herb on the square. Seven o'clock on the dot to discuss how this is going to go down. Be there or forget it." I shrugged his arm off of mine and left.

PLAYLIST

Can't get enough DTF and want to keep rocking out? Check out a few songs from the official *On the Rox* playlist below. For the full playlist, visit Spotify and search for Kat Addams and keep on rocking.

"Roxanne" | The Police

"I Love Rock 'n' Roll" | Joan Jett & the Blackhearts

"Blackbird" | The Beatles

"Everlong" | Foo Fighters

"Love at First Sight" | The Brobecks

"Broken" | Seether, featuring Amy Lee

"Shimmer" | Fuel

"I'm Like a Bird" | Nelly Furtado

"Raven" | Jewel

"Sunshine of Your Love" | Cream

"Kintsugi" | Gabrielle Aplin

ACKNOWLEDGMENTS

To my daughter, my world. I hope you know how strong you are and that you always know your worth. All the stars in the sky can't come close to outshining you. You are my reason. For everything.

Thank you to my editor, Jovana Shirley, and my cover designer, Lori Jackson. You two make my books sparkle! I'm so glad I found the best in the industry to hold my hand through this crazy process of writing!

And lastly, thank you to my Bettys, my Nikkis, my Laylas, and especially my Jays. Your support has been life-changing.

ARE YOU OR SOMEONE YOU KNOW
EXPERIENCING ABUSE?

PLEASE, GET HELP TODAY.
YOU DESERVE LOVE.

US: National Domestic Violence Hotline
1-800-799-7233

Canada: Domestic Violence Hotline 1-866-863-0511

Australia: Domestic Violence Hotline 1800 737 732

United Kingdom: Domestic Violence Hotline
0808 2000 247

ABOUT THE AUTHOR

Kat Addams is a forever twenty-nine-year-old fashionista following her lifelong dream of writing contemporary romance inspired by the exotic men she meets in her worldly travels. At least, that's what she would like for you to think. She's certainly not a stay-at-home mom indulging in excessive daydreaming, frozen pizzas, an unhealthy addiction to purchasing pajamas, and one too many cocktails on the regular. That's some other romance author. The poor thing probably has to sneak away upstairs to write her dirty stories! What would her family think? Thankfully, that's not Kat!

Social Media:

Still crazy about Kat? Rawr! Stalk her on the social media platforms linked below!

> https://linktr.ee/author_kat_addams
>
> (For all of the links in one convenient location!)
>
> Newsletter: https://kataddams.com/free-book
>
> (Bonus *Hotty Toddy* Free E-Book)

Want to keep up with all the mischief and bad decisions? Be sure to subscribe to Kat's newsletter for the latest news. By becoming a subscriber, you'll be the first to know the juicy details on upcoming releases! You'll also be the first to hear of special offers, exclusive content, sneak peeks, terrible ideas, ridiculous shenanigans, and more! As a special gift for signing up, you'll also receive a free e-book, *Hotty Toddy*. Check below for more information on this stand-alone, second chance, and fake marriage novella.

> Goodreads:
> www.goodreads.com/author/show/19253462.Kat_Addams
>
> Bookbub:
> www.bookbub.com/profile/kat-addams
>
> Amazon:
> http://amazon.com/author/kataddams

DTF, Dirty. Tough. Females. (A Kat Addams Reader Group): https://www.facebook.com/groups/ DirtyToughFemales/

(A Facebook group to stay connected, laugh, and share. Hope to see you there!)

Facebook: www.facebook.com/KatAddamsAuthor

Instagram: www.instagram.com/authorkataddams

Twitter: https://twitter.com/KatAddamsAuthor

ARC Team: https://docs.google.com/forms/u/2/d/e /1FAIpQLScinoImFEIChW3PQ4_BrlBo YxpcClYTftNZRz-1DmI- 121R8A/viewform?usp=send_form

(Interested in receiving Kat Addams's latest books before release? Click the link to join the ARC team!)

OTHER BOOKS BY KAT ADDAMS

DIRTY SOUTH SERIES

Hotty Toddy (Free for newsletter subscribers:
https://kataddams.com/free-book)

Grit and Grind

Nashvegas Nights

Mr. Big Ego

Mayday

DTF (DIRTY. TOUGH. FEMALE.) SERIES

On the Rox

Cream-Pied

Whip It Out

Just the Tip